PRAISE FOR

ugly to start with

"I can't wait to pass this book along."

—Susan Straight, author of seven novels, including *Highwire Moon*,
a finalist for the National Book Award

"Lovely, funny, melancholy."

—Maxine Chernoff, author of *A Boy in Winter*

"These stories are spare and direct, resisting the pyrotechnics of language in order to concentrate on the much more important task of reaching for emotional truth."

—Gary Fincke, author of *The History of Permanence*

"Pitch-perfect West Virginia voices."

—Enid Shomer, author of *Tourist Season: Stories*

"Like Faulkner, Cummings knows the strong undertow that blood exerts on ambition and self-preservation."

—Charlotte Holmes, short story writer and essayist published in
Epoch, New Letters, Story, and *The New Yorker*.

"Sparkling, deeply intelligent, and often heartbreakingly funny."

—Eileen Pollack, author of *The Rabbit in the Attic*,
In the Mouth, and *Paradise*

"Like Huck Finn and Holden Caulfield, John Michael Cummings' teenage narrator reveals the troubled and tender and tough heart of a place both split and knit by class, race, and family."

—Wayne Karlin, author of *Wandering Souls: Journeys With the Dead
and the Living in Viet Nam* and *Prisoners*

Vandalia Press, Morgantown 26505

Copyright 2011 John Michael Cummings

First edition published 2011 by Vandalia Press

Printed in the United States of America

Vandalia Press is an imprint of West Virginia University Press

16 15 14 13 12 11   9 8 7 6 5 4 3 2 1

ISBN:

Paper: 978-1-935978-08-4 (alk. paper)

E-book: 978-1-935978-09-1

Library of Congress Cataloguing-in-Publication Data

Ugly to Start With/John Michael Cummings

p.   cm.

In process

The stories in *Ugly to Start With* were previously published in the following journals: "The World Around Us," *Northwords*, Fall 2003, Issue 32; "Two Tunes," *Rosebud*, 2003, Issue 28; "Ugly To Start With," *The Bitter Oleander*, 2003, vol. 9, no. 1; "The Fence," *Confrontation*, No. 82/83 Spring/Summer 2003; "We Never Liked Them Anyway," *Concho River Review*, Vol. 18, No. 2; "The Wallet," *Salt River Review*, Vol. 7, No. 3, Fall 2004; "Rusty Clackford," *Oyez Review*, Spring 2008; "Mountain Wake," *The Foliate Oak*, April 2007; "John Brown the Quaker," *Global City Review*, Spring/Summer 2008; "Carter," *Passager*, issue 37; "Indians and Teddy Bears Were Here First," *The Cortland Review*, Issue 36; "The Scratchboard Project," *The Iowa Review*, issue 36, no. 1; "Generations," *Stirring: A Literary Collection*, Vol. 9, Edition 2, 2007

Book Design by Than Saffel

Background cover art by Betty Gannon *http://www.bettygannon.com/*

Silhouette image by Perforex *http:// perforex.deviantart.com/*

Author photo by Angie Cope

John Michael Cummings

ugly to start with

Vandalia Press

MORGANTOWN 2011

To the memory of my brother Joe

Contents

The World Around Us

∗ ∗ ∗

On our way back from town, Mom and I spotted Ernesto, the new artist in Harpers Ferry, walking along the highway. We shot past, and I begged her to stop. She looked at me as if for the life of her she couldn't understand me. Then, she took her foot off the gas and began signaling over.

"I don't know about this, Jason," she said.

I stuck my head out the window and peered back down the highway. Ernesto was trying to catch up, but the large sheets of paper he was carrying in the grip of one hand bent in the wind whenever he hurried. I told Mom to back the car up, but she said that was too dangerous to do on the shoulder.

He reached us at last.

"Jason?" he said, smiling.

He knew me from the streets of Harpers Ferry, where I was always following the artists around. Then he looked in at my mother, and I turned and watched her look at him for the first time.

He had difficulty fitting the large paper into the backseat, so my mother offered to open the trunk. But he solved the problem by bowing the paper until it fit between the seats. Then he squeezed himself in to one side, and Mom pulled away as if we were now hauling something fragile.

Everyone was quiet at first. I looked back. He had that same warm smile and tanned face under white stubble.

"It is nice of you, Jason," he said, "to have your mother stop."

His accent. It always made me think of someplace far away, and that was strange, imagining a faraway place while in our old West Virginia car.

"Were you just back at Merrimack's?" my mother asked, glancing in the mirror.

I was turned around in the seat so that I could watch both him and Mom without moving.

He said he must confess that he did not know what "Merrimack's" was.

"Our office supply in town?"

"Yes, of course," he said, smiling.

I saw a gold tooth in the corner of his mouth. He said something else, but it was lost in the sound of air coming in the window.

Mom wound up her window a little.

"They have a nice selection there, don't they?" she said. "My son gets all his art supplies there."

"Yes, Jason likes art," he said. "That is very good, Jason. You must show me your work sometime."

I kept looking at him. His voice was full of strange, beautiful sounds.

"Jason has always had an interest in drawing," Mom said, speaking up toward the mirror as if it were a microphone attached to a speaker in the backseat. "He gets it from his father."

I looked over. Why did she have to say that?

"His father is an artist?" Ernesto asked.

"Well, no, not exactly. He painted some years ago, when he was younger."

I thought of my father, not so young any more, working this afternoon and every afternoon, doing nothing with his life.

"My father was also very talented," Ernesto said. "He made little statuettes out of alabaster."

"Oh, are you from Italy then?" Mom said.

"Yes, Florence."

"Oh, how beautiful."

"You have been there?"

"Oh no, but I've seen pictures."

For my mother, pictures were as good as the real thing. She had a coffee table book of Italian pottery, which included the pictures she was talking about.

"This," Ernesto said, looking out the car window at the hills outside Charles Town, "reminds me of the northern vineyards in Tuscany."

Mom let her foot off the gas. "*This?* Jefferson County?"

The only other time she let her foot off the gas was when she remembered something she had forgotten to get at the grocery store for Dad.

"There is a slight resemblance, yes," he said.

Mom looked sick—Jefferson County resembling the beautiful vineyards in some far-off land?

I was surprised she was acting this way. She always said how beautiful our county was and always talked about how awful it was that the National Park Service was taking over all the farmlands. I thought she would like hearing that our county was as beautiful as some far-off place. But she was looking in the mirror at Ernesto as if she didn't need to see the road anymore.

"I was surprised," he said, leaning forward so that we could hear him, "to find out that they have no bus service in this region."

"Oh, no, nothing like that," Mom said back. Her face was full of questions. "Are you staying here in town?"

"Yes," he said, "at the Hill House. I am with a group of teachers from the Corcoran."

"Oh, the Corcoran Art Institute? I've certainly heard of that."

"Yes, well, we thought the hotel would provide shuttle service. Then, I was told it was only a few miles to that town." He laughed a little.

"Oh, no," Mom said, "Charles Town is too far to walk. It's a full eight miles."

She was embarrassing with her little facts. So what if it was eight miles? I looked out at the cornfields.

Actually, how far it was from Harpers Ferry to Charles Town had been a little matter of dispute in our family. The signs said eight, Dad said six, our speedometer said five, sometimes seven, but everyone else, including Grandma, thought it was at least ten. And for some reason, the county, when they made this new highway, didn't put in all the mile markers. So we settled on eight miles, since Mom couldn't imagine that the county would make such a mistake in math.

"You have been to the Corcoran?" Ernesto asked her.

"Oh, once," she said, "but long ago."

I looked over. "You did?"

"With my mother," she said, not to me but to Ernesto. "But that's been years."

"I was about to ask," he said, leaning forward some more, "do the school children in this region go into the city, to visit the museums?"

"Oh, no," Mom said back, as if he had just asked her something that around here no one ever questioned, like why the liquor stores weren't open on Sunday.

"But why not?" he asked.

Mom and I looked at each other.

"It seems a short drive to the city."

"Oh no," Mom said, "it's sixty-five miles."

That was something else in question. The sign at Harpers Ferry said sixty-five miles to Washington, D.C., but the one in Charles Town said seventy-six, which couldn't be right if it was eight miles from Harpers Ferry to Charles Town.

Once, we tried to check the distance between Harpers Ferry and Charles Town using Mom's wristwatch. My brother Andy knew from science class that when we were going sixty miles per hour, we were going a mile a minute. So we timed it and ended up with twelve minutes. But that wasn't really accurate either, because half the time Mom was afraid to go the full five mph over the speed limit, to say nothing of how many times she kept getting stuck behind slow cars. So we settled on sixty-five miles, just as we had settled on eight miles, because that's what the sign closest to Harpers Ferry said and because it was the easier number for everyone to remember, being exactly ten above the speed limit.

However many miles away the city was, it wasn't far. If you shut your eyes and counted, it was counting to sixty, sixty times. If you went by minutes, it was only a little more than an hour, and a little more than an hour was nothing, just "Bewitched" and "I Dream of Jeannie" back to back.

"Yes, I suppose it is a long drive," Ernesto said.

I looked over at Mom. "It's only an hour."

"Oh, Jason, it's longer than that," she said.

I gave her a quick glare. The city wasn't far for tourists or for anyone who wasn't afraid to drive to new places. Dad tried to say that the tires on our car were too old for long trips. But we could have taken the Amtrak or the Greyhound out of Frederick to the city. It wasn't the old tires. It was us.

And as far as it taking "longer" to get to the city, Mom was thinking back to when the roads between here and there were all twisted up and narrow and you couldn't go fast or pass, when they all had double lines and "Road Narrows" signs everywhere.

Today, though, there were brand-new car bridges around town and a new highway all the way to Frederick, where there were even bigger roads that led to the city.

This highway we were on was new. Whenever we took it to the shopping mall in Frederick, we saw more and more signs for Washington, D.C. and Baltimore. Mom called it "the metropolitan area." There was a jumble of ramps and overpasses, everything crossing and crisscrossing, somehow coming together, then branching out in every direction. It terrified her.

I looked over at her, determined to win our little argument, even if there was somebody else in the car.

"Dr. Reynolds said it takes an hour," I said. He didn't really say this, but she didn't know.

"Well, he probably drives too fast," she said back.

"It takes Mr. Powell an hour," I said right back.

She gave me an impatient look. "Jason, I know it takes longer. Now stop."

It took Greg Lucas's father only an hour by Amtrak. A couple of times he even took a bus from Frederick, and that took even less time.

Mom looked in the mirror at Ernesto and said with that kind of smile that only made me madder: "I don't know where my son gets these ideas."

"It's twenty minutes to Frederick, Mom—you said so!"

I didn't mean to raise my voice. But she couldn't argue with me about that. We had timed that, too. About twenty minutes for twenty-two miles, or a mile a minute.

She looked out at the roadway, at the dashes that passed us every millisecond.

"Well, I guess you're right," she said, "cause it's another forty miles or so beyond that."

Ernesto leaned forward and said in his thick, Italian voice, "As I understand it, the proximity of Harpers Ferry to Washington, D.C. was its value in the Civil War, and that led to the arsenal being erected there."

Mom didn't know what to say to this.

"What he means, Mom," I said, rolling my eyes, "is that it was always close."

She gave me a sharp look. But I ignored her, opened the glove box, and took out the Texaco map. I spread the map out on my lap, despite her telling me to put it away because the wind would just blow it around. I knew just where to find Harpers Ferry on it. It was written in italics, as *Harpers Ferry Historic National Park,* and was crowded in by places I had never heard of before, places apparently right beside me all my life. Cumberland Village. New Brighton. Kingston. Rt. 340 was nothing more than an itty-bitty blue line that went nowhere by itself. It ran into a zillion bigger blue and red lines that twisted around and met with other blue and red lines that came in from everywhere. According to this, the city was all around us. Washington, D.C. was half a pinky away, and the Atlantic Ocean was not much farther. We could see Baltimore, even Philadelphia. I couldn't believe all the thick roads. I-270, 495, 95 North. On and on. There was this huge, filled up world all around us that I couldn't see.

Mom went on looking straight ahead. We were coming up on the Harpers Ferry exit. Here the highway seemed especially wide and sunny. I liked the feeling of the world coming through here. Around us were trucks from Virginia and Pennsylvania. I even saw a sports car with Delaware plates. Lying along the shoulders were burnt up, fallen-off mufflers and shreds of truck tires, stuff that made the highway seem like a racetrack every car and truck in America was on.

I turned around in the seat.

"What are you gonna draw?" I asked.

He looked at me as if it took a moment to bring his mind back from wherever it was.

"This is for a project I have planned, Jason. A drawing of the Lockwood House."

Mom changed her grip on the steering wheel. "I'm sorry you had to walk so far."

"Oh, I do not mind," Ernesto said. "The countryside here is so beautiful."

She looked up in the mirror. "You really think West Virginia looks like Tuscany?"

He smiled and nodded.

Two Tunes

* * *

My family felt the whole house tense up that morning Marty
Howell pushed the front door all the way open just by knocking
on it. The brick that had been behind the door, holding it slightly
open so that smoke from the wood stove could clear out, slid off
the step and clunked on the floor. Dad, half behind the door, half
in front of it, trying to tuck in his shirt while holding a gun behind his back, had do a little dance to keep from having the brick
tumble over on his toe.

Just like that, Marty was inside our house. He was probably
the only man in town who could kick my father's ass. A few years
back, he had taught karate up at the Jefferson Training Center on
Wednesday nights. But in this situation, that didn't seem to matter. Nor did it matter that he was my history teacher at the junior
high school, or that he was a park ranger in town in the evenings
and on weekends, or that he was a local boy. No one came into our
house. All of Harpers Ferry knew that. Dad's rule. Maybe Grandma
Jennings came in, if we let her, but nobody else. Maybe Uncle
Dave, too. Dad *had* to let him in, not because he was his brother,
but because he had let him in from the start. That was the only way
anyone got into our house, by having done it before.

Dad told us he didn't want anyone seeing his precious, restored guns. Word would get out to the wrong people, he said. But the real reason was he was ashamed of the house, of how small it was and especially of the condition of the kitchen, with its rotted plasterboard walls and wet-stained ceiling from a leak around the commode upstairs—problems he could have fixed if he had just put his mind to it, Mom said.

Our front porch had a real hillbilly look, too, but that in itself was never a problem. We had a maple tree out front to keep tourists from seeing the dirty plastic covering the windows, the white extension cord holding up the rain gutter, and the junk stacked everywhere. We had that tree to hide the heaps of ugly firewood thrown up on the porch and the Band-Aid tan paint Dad mixed from several leftover paints and used on the porch railing and window trim. We had that tree to cover the strange damp stain across the rock face of our house, a stain somehow caused by the moldy hillside behind us. We had that tree to cover up our dog Barfy, too—named for what he did best, running the flower bed bare, choking himself on his own chain, then throwing up. We had a tree for all this. One big tree.

What we didn't have was a way to cover up the raw sewage smell. Dad had put our sewage line in himself years ago, but he built it above ground, using plastic pipes that not only came apart when Barfy stepped on them but, when the sun shined on them, were see-through. If you were on our front porch when someone flushed the toilet, not only could you hear water flowing all around, but you could see gray shapes running through the pipes, especially around the elbows, where the stuff got slowed down. Sometimes we'd come outside and find the pipes knocked apart and blue Charmin tissue all over the ground and that smell in the air. Whenever this happened, Mom threw down peat moss to try to cover everything up.

With Marty Howell in our house, I barely had enough time to scramble up the stairs and out of sight. My brothers were already waiting for me at the top.

"It ain't me this time," Andy, the oldest, whispered first. He looked at me, the youngest, then at Greg. "What'd you do, Greg?"

It was a kind of game we played when trouble was near, one of us blaming the other first, as if by being blamed and by the rules of the game, that person was guilty.

"It's not me," Greg said back.

No, it probably wasn't Greg. All he ever did was exactly what Dad told him, while showing an aptitude for everything Dad admired, from sharpening saw blades to identifying different kinds of trees.

Andy looked at me, his eyes widening. "Jason!"

I couldn't say it wasn't me because lately I had lost track of the things I had done wrong. But we didn't have much time to point fingers. Downstairs, Dad was going into his "personality routine." That's what we called it, when he tried to be all smiles and jokes. It was his disguise, his way to make himself seem happy when inside he was as ornery and twisted up as a piece of petrified hickory— twisted up from all those years working at the post office and living among tourists in Harpers Ferry.

He was talking loud, too. That was his way of alerting Mom to keep the kitchen door shut so that Marty couldn't see in.

When I began crawling down the stairs on my stomach like an alligator, Andy and Greg backed up. As I peered down into the living room, I saw Marty's tall body cramped down under our low ceiling. Every time he started talking, he'd stand up straight, and when his ranger hat hit our ceiling, mashing down over his head, he'd duck down again.

He was the tallest ranger in Harpers Ferry, and we were the shortest family. We lived in an armory worker's house, which were known to be small, so small you could cross our living room in three, maybe four stretched-out steps. Our kitchen was half that size. Marty could cross in two at most. There was nothing else on the first floor, just these two small rooms stuck together, and a sticky old back door that, like the front door, popped like a can of vacuum-sealed peanuts whenever opened.

"Bill, all your blinds are drawn," Marty was saying, with an annoyed glance toward the ceiling, "I wasn't sure you were home."

Our blinds were always drawn. Marty knew that. He was just embarrassed for having lurched his long legs into our small house without being asked. He might have played in our backyard as a boy, but he had never been in our house before today. He knew better.

Dad picked up the brick and placed it out of the way. Then he gave the front door a shove, shutting it tight. In his other hand was his gun. Dad held it out for Marty to see. He clicked the safety on.

"Marty," he said, "you know how things have gotten down here. We've had damn tourists trying to walk right in on us."

He handed the gun to Marty by its grip, and Marty looked it over, impressed by the grooves and thick barrel.

"They come right up to our door," Dad went on, "thinking we're another shop. Why, just the other day, a damn fellow, I think he saw all my guns and figured this was a gun shop. Well, I grabbed my .45—that Army model right there—and I yelled, 'Here, get the hell out, you son-of-a-bitch, this is a private residence!'" He broke into his wheezing, pipe smoker's laugh. "You should have seen that bugger run!"

It almost seemed to be a show-business routine, the way he carried on, getting people a little afraid, bewildered, and grinning all at the same time. You wanted to step back, because everything he said, every question he asked, and every look on his face, all seemed to be leading you into a big practical joke.

Marty grinned along with Dad, but it was a cautious grin.

"You should put up a sign, Bill," he said, sounding official as he took off his hat. His head was a pink ball, completely bald, even though he was still young.

"Well, we did that, Marty," Dad said back, with the tone of standing up for himself. "But those damn niggers tore it down."

Dad used the n-word a lot and figured he could say it in front of Marty, since he was a local boy. Dad's whole side of the family used that word. Grandma Stevens even called black dogs that word. Mom didn't like the word, and I didn't either. But I knew what Dad was complaining about. Washington folks came into our town on big silver buses with the Capitol plates and started traipsing around, littering, and being loud. You could tell they were from the city, too, because of how clumsily they walked up and down our hilly streets, as if they had never been off level ground before. The kids shoplifted from Mr. Johnston's shop and ran around in the street in front of our house with green and orange water guns that had nothing to do with the Civil War. Or they flew those whirligigs into the side of our house, and then ran up onto our porch to try to get them back. Sometimes Dad flung the door open and yelled for the little sons of bitches to get off his property, the whole time holding his Army .45 behind his back. That was exciting.

Marty handed the gun back to Dad, and Dad laid it on his workbench. Local boy or not, Marty Howell was here for a reason, and it couldn't be a good one. But it was up to Marty to say why. That was Dad being clever, playing poker with the conversation. Dad gave Marty a long second or two, and when he didn't say anything, he rapped on the front door until our stupid dog stopping barking, and then had Marty sit on the chest in front of the workbench.

The chest was an obvious seat. Dad liked having Grandma sit on it, on account of what was in it—half a dozen dud grenades, different kinds of combat knives, live bullets for machine guns, and other war things my father had brought back from the Korean War, including brass knuckles. It gave him a weird thrill to have Grandma on Mom's side sit on all these things.

I lay on my stomach in the stairs, peering around.

"Marty, you've never seen my guns, have you?"

Dad knew he hadn't. He was rubbing it in. He took one of his rifles off the wall. There were at least two dozen of them hanging around the room, from a 1689 flintlock musket made somewhere in England to a 1921 Lansing fowling piece last owned by Howard Taft's granddaughter, supposedly.

But the gun he took off the wall was made right here in Harpers Ferry, he was telling Marty. An 1858 Harpers Ferry breechloader, one of the first hundred of its type ever made. He handed it to Marty and told him to read the serial number etched into a plate on the end of the stock.

"00037—this is the 37th one, Bill?" asked Marty.

Dad gave him a smug grin. Marty might had gone off to that teacher's college for a few years, but he still didn't know the history of the town the way my father did. Harpers Ferry was important for one reason: its armory that manufactured the first American breechloaders.

Some years ago, a fellow high up in the Park had offered Dad a lot of money for the Harpers Ferry breechloader. But Dad refused and to this day enjoyed still refusing. When there were no tourists in town, he walked down to the Master Armorer's House just to enjoy seeing how much worse their breechloader looked under glass than his hanging up on our wall. Theirs was missing a trigger guard and had deep chips in the stock. Not only that, it was no-where near the 37th one ever made.

Marty, naturally, was impressed by the good condition of the gun, and Dad went on to explain to him what a breechloader was, even if he already knew. Even showed him where it was loaded. Then, out of nowhere, like before, came a knock on our door. Up came our stupid dog again, out of the bushes, lunging and carrying on. I backed up the steps a little.

My father, holding up his hand to tell Marty to sit still, went to the door instead, lifted a single Venetian blind, and peered through. He always went to the door this way. Then he opened the door with the same smooth, silent swiftness that he slid back the bolts on his rifles.

Pat Kennedy was at our door. She was another park ranger, a woman ranger. Dad cared even less for those.

I was surprised she started inside our house on her own, as if it was another park building to patrol, and even more surprised that Dad stepped aside for her. Of course it was because Marty was al-ready inside that she acted as if she belonged inside, too.

Thinking herself funny, she asked Dad if he was going to church this morning. Everyone knew that Dad didn't like any of the churches in town. He didn't like the priests. Too liberal, he said.

"Pat, tell me something," Dad said, looking put upon as he shut the door again, "why in the hell did you want to become a park ranger?"

He went on to make it sound like the worst decision a woman could make. You see, my family had a real problem with park rang-ers. They had a problem with us, too. Except for Marty, they didn't know us, we didn't know them, and no one made a move in either direction. They rode around in their jeeps, acting important, setting up sawhorses here and there, rerouting traffic for no good reason, making life difficult on residents like us.

Pat kept her hat on as she stood looking around. She had ignored my father's question and looked all the stronger for having done so. He was bent over, clearing the sofa of guns to make room for her. He didn't look happy about being forced to put his prized breechloader on the floor.

No one much cared for Pat. Mom said she was pushy, but the real problem was she was a woman in a man's job. For that reason, Mom would never come out of the kitchen now. Andy and Greg had probably scrambled out on the roof by now.

I watched her sit. To the rest of the world, it was a secret that this sofa folded out into my parents' bed at night. That was another reason Dad didn't want anyone in the house. He didn't want strangers sitting around where he and Mom slept. A long time ago, Mom had wanted Dad to add onto the house, but he said he didn't mind sleeping on the foldaway bed where it was. That way, he could keep an eye on the house, which meant he could keep an eye on his guns. Anyone who broke in would have to come by him first.

Pat sat a moment to take it all in—we had as many wall clocks as guns: old round clocks with fancy Roman numerals, newer rectangular ones with small gold pendulums, and smaller clocks on the mantle, including one that looked like Monticello. There was a grandfather clock in the corner, tall enough to hold a mummy, and a cuckoo clock above Marty with the little bird stuck halfway out of its door. All these clocks had stopped years ago—stopped at different times: twenty minutes after three, five after five, and one with both hands dead on the twelve.

Guns and clocks. Pat looked amused. She kept looking around, as if trying to find a message. Her eyes stopped dead on the kitchen

Two Tunes

door. Being a maple-stained, slatted door, new and modern compared to the plain white plasterboard walls around it, it drew attention to itself. In this situation, it had an intentionally shut look.

"How many rooms in this house, Mr. Stevens?" she asked, eyes still on the kitchen door.

That was the start of them, her poking, long-nosed, big-eyed questions. She looked at the low ceiling. How old was the house? 200 years old? Everything she saw led to another question. A wood stove? The house was heated by firewood? Solely by firewood?

"Is that a church pew?"

We had a church pew in our living room. It came water-damaged from St. Peter's sometime in the '50s. Dad restored it himself. We called it the "pumpkin bench" because of its pumpkin-colored cushion.

Soon enough Pat's big eyes crossed the floor and headed in my direction, like something coming up the stairs after me. There was an upstairs? A third floor, too?

With Marty sitting on a chest of explosives and Pat on the foldaway bed, my father looked helpless, answering her questions. He didn't tell her that the third floor was unheated, because of a bad flue up there, so there was really no third floor at all, at least not for living in.

Around the living room were enough war relics for her to notice, from powder horns and canteens to bayonets and a bugle, including a pair of derringers and crisscrossing cavalry swords.

She looked over at Marty. "*We* should have all this on exhibit," she said.

That was the wrong remark for Dad to hear, and especially the wrong tone.

"I know why you two are here," he said, standing up straight and giving them both a look.

My father could change fast, his face going from a dozen faint smiles to one strong frown.

Marty, at this point, spoke up: "Superintendent Keith asked us—"

"I know what he wants," Dad interrupted. "Got a damn letter from him last month. 'Superintendent Keith?' Humph, you mean Dick Keith."

"Mr. Stevens—" Pat began, but Dad cut her off, too.

"You people have wanted this house for a long time now, and now you're up to something again."

They couldn't argue with him on that one. Lately the town was becoming even more famous, thanks to Senator Byrd, and the Park was buying property all around town. They had already taken Learner's orchard because supposedly the land was the site of the Virginia militia's surrender to Lee, or something like that. Dad said that eventually, whether Mom liked it or not, we, too, would have to find another place to live.

The Park could force us to sell, he said. They could give us a good offer, and we'd have to take it. "Eminent domain." He said these two words as if they were the nastiest two in the language.

Recently, the Park had begun fixing up buildings on Hanmore Street, claiming that they were part of the first black college or some such thing. Important to "black heritage," they said. You don't want to know what Dad had to say about that.

He walked over to the workbench where Marty was sitting and picked up a bright white letter that lay folded on top of one of his Pogo cartoon books.

"A damn information summons," he said, turning. "Suppose 'Superintendent Keith' sent you down here to find out why I haven't sent it back yet?" Having slowed the situation down to his pace, he held up the letter and read aloud parts of what sounded like a questionnaire. "'Total acreage?' 'Dimensions?' 'Date of con-struction?'" He looked at both of them. "You'd think you'd already know this, since the house is so damn important to you." He went on. "'Department of the Interior, Acquisitions'." Then he pointed at the kitchen door and said in a low voice, "*She's* the one who wants to keep this damn place. I don't."

Actually, Mom's reasoning was, even if we had to sell, we didn't necessarily have to move out of town. We could live closer to her parents, where the Park wasn't interested in buying land. But for Dad that was out of the question.

"If it's that valuable to you, Mr. Stevens," Pat started saying, with attitude, "why don't you get an attorney?"

"Goddamn attorneys," he said.

He opened the small door to the storage space under the stairs and stepped in—directly under me. I heard him move boxes around and felt vibrations through the stairs. When he switched on the light, it shot through the cracks between the steps and striped my arms and shirt. As far as I knew, there was nothing under the stairs except about ten years of *Guns & Ammo* magazines. Andy said there was a *Playboy* among them, but we never found it.

While he rummaged around, he kept talking to Marty, telling him how damn difficult it was living in Harpers Ferry with all the tourists. They blocked our driveway, standing in it to look across the street at the windows of the John Brown Wax Museum.

"Why don't you call an attorney, Bill?" said Marty.

"Call" was an impossible word in our house, since ours was probably the only house in town that, for the longest while, didn't have a phone. That was because Dad was unreasonable about it, Mom always said. His excuse was that if we had a phone, every damn character on his mail route would be calling him, wanting to know when their disability checks would arrive.

Just then, out of the corner of my eye, I saw the kitchen door open. Mom!

"William, I don't mean to interrupt—hi, Pat, Marty."

My mother always gave others the warmest smiles. She got her politeness from her mother and didn't let Dad take it away.

"Katie, you're not interrupting," Dad said, coming out of the storage space, already annoyed with her. "I've been waiting for you to get in on this."

"Well, William, you know how I feel." She looked at Marty and Pat. "I'm sorry, but I just don't want to move." Mom loved being in the center of the historic district of Harpers Ferry.

Pat gave her a sympathetic look.

"Well, shit," my father said, making himself seem mean.

Marty spoke up. "You don't have to move. You can apply for a merchant's reprieve."

All we had to do, he said, was to put some sort of shop in the house and the Park couldn't force us to sell. That was what Mrs. Hall had done.

Dad laughed, and that was the end of that suggestion.

Mom was still up on the kitchen step, unsure whether to step down into the small living room. She looked a little nervous, too, standing in front of so many people, but she handled herself better than I would have.

"Pat, I saw your mother in Acme the other day," she said. "She always looks so lovely."

I loved this about my mother, how she could go from sadness to pleasantness with one great push from the inside.

Pat smiled. "Well, thank you, Mrs. Stevens," she said. "Yes, Mom knows how to take care of herself. I hope I look as good as she does at her age."

They both laughed.

"Oh, I'm sure you will, Pat."

Behind Pat Kennedy's back, Mom always said that Pat needed to lose weight and that being overweight ages a person.

"Your husband was just showing us some of his things. They sure are nice."

"Yes, Pat, they sure are," my mother said in a slightly different voice. "And as you can see, the room is full of them."

They both laughed again.

My mother's manners were like something out of an old-fashioned book. Not that she came from a rich family or went beyond high school. But on her side of the family, everyone was civil to one another. Civil. That was the word she used. "At least we're *civil* to one another, Bill," she said, in defense of them.

Andy, who was pretty smart, said the big difference between Mom and Dad was that she was English and Dad was Irish. The English were like whites in our county, the Irish like blacks. He also said that Mom was the unlucky daughter in her family, marrying Dad. You could sure see that in Granddaddy Roy's face.

But as second-class as Dad made Mom, she was still polite and kind to everyone, and you couldn't help but be nice back. She had that effect on people, as if she instantly gave everyone around her good manners, sprinkled on them as if by a good witch. With Mom in the room, Pat Kennedy, of all people, was behaving herself as a woman should.

"What a gorgeous musket, Mr. Stevens," she said.

"Now, it's not a musket, Pat," he said, reaching and taking it down for her to see. Dad was acting different, too. Better. "It's a rifle. There's a difference. Katie knows all about it." He gave my mother a strange little smile before placing the gun on Pat's lap. She grimaced a little from the weight of it.

While he explained the process of rifling, my mother tried to find a place for herself in the small room. She said hello to Marty as she stepped off the kitchen step and sat on the pumpkin bench. I never saw her sit there before. She didn't look comfortable, with her legs, like mine when I sat there, barely reaching the floor.

"Marty, how's Debbie?" she asked, in a tone that didn't distract Dad as he went on with his give-Pat-the-royal-treatment routine now.

"She's fine, Katie," Marty said back. "Busy as usual."

Marty didn't sound like himself, either. His voice sounded soft. That was the effect Mom had on men.

When Dad finished explaining the process, he took his pride and joy carefully from Pat's lap by handling it by the stock so as not to put his fingerprints on the oiled barrel. Then he laid it across a cane chair, reached up, and took a similar-looking gun down off the wall.

"Now this is a muzzle-loader," he said. "It's loaded from up at the end of the barrel, the muzzle."

Mom looked on, with slight amusement on her face. I often saw this look, but never understood it. Something about my father was funny to her.

Pat was suddenly more interested in Dad's steel lap guitar in the corner. It was something Dad had ordered out of a catalog. He had even taught himself to play. Not that the steel guitar was difficult to play, he said. It was easier than the regular guitar and a hell of a lot easier than the fiddle.

He picked it up, blew off the dust, and stepped over to his workbench with it where he dug out his pick and sliding metal bar. Then he sat on the pumpkin bench beside Mom and put it across his lap. That was *two* nevers. He never sat on the pumpkin bench, and he never sat beside Mom like that.

He picked a few strings, then brought his hand down on them, silencing them. My father was rarely in a good mood, and now that he was heading in that direction, more or less, he made us all wait.

"This is banjo country, Bill," said Pat—it was okay for her to call him Bill now. "What are you doing with that . . ."

"It's Hawaiian, Pat," he said.

"Hawaiian?"

He nodded and took up a serious expression. With any guitar, he said, it was all about strumming and chord voicing, as they called it. Pat watched with fascination as he put his ear down to the strings and strummed, first fast, then string by string. He said he didn't think it was tuned quite right, but it probably didn't matter, as long as it was tuned to an open chord.

Mom reached down into the case and took out what was left—a booklet—and handed it to Pat.

"'Musical theory'?" she said, leafing through it. "Bill, you? Meter, treble, and bass clefs—you?"

Now I understood that amused look Mom had. Pat had it, too.

"With any string instrument," my father said, putting on a pick, "it's all about melody. One note at a time. That's melody." A person who played the piano, for example, had to deal with many notes at once. That was harmony.

"Melody? Harmony?" said Pat. "'I only know two tunes; one is 'Yankee Doodle' and the other isn't'—you know who said that?" She looked over at Marty, but was asking either man.

"Ulysses S. Grant," my father said.

Pat's big face lit up as pink as Marty's head, and she watched in amazement as Dad picked a string and at the same time slid the bar up and back. It made that classic guitar twang, plus more. He did this several times, and the sounds came together into a tune.

"Katie?" she said, looking at Mom. Her mouth hung open.

"I know, Pat."

Dad started playing faster, looking as if figuring it out as he went, and before long he had the three of them smiling and glancing around at each other. Then he made a screech with the steel bar, and Pat said what he needed was sheet music. Both Dad and Marty shook their heads at the same time. Folk music was learned by ear, they said. Anything above a C8 was useless anyway, my father added, unless you were writing a damn symphony.

"I just let my hand wander."

He plucked a few strings and with the steel bar pulled on the sounds like taffy. Other sounds he kept short and high-pitched and all whipped up near his fingers. Pat was grinning like crazy. So was I.

Dad stopped to say that any number of objects could be used to make the slide sound. The neck of a bottle. Anything. That was how the sound became popular. B.B. King, he said. Everyone had heard of him.

He reached over and picked up a metal file off his workbench and put the big dirty thing against the shiny strings. When the same fine sound came out, Pat practically jumped her big butt off the sofa she was so tickled. Marty's pink head was pinker than ever.

Dad stopped, dug into his baggy pocket, and took out his penknife. He handed it to Mom who opened it for him and handed it back. Then he lay the blade against the strings. It was called "singing" or "resonating," he said. Hawaiians first used an ordinary railroad spike.

He went into a jazzy tune, plucking and sliding, and Marty, suddenly in a crazy mood, stood up and grabbed Pat by the hands and made her stand up, too, and before she could push him away and say he was acting foolish, he got out a few clown-like dance steps with her. Everyone laughed—two park rangers in their green uniforms, dancing in our little living room. Mom was in stitches.

"Marty remembers this," Dad said, calming things down. He hit a few strings.

I remembered it, too. Mom always said I was too young to remember. When Marty was about Andy's age, which would have made me three, he came down to our house after school and played in the dump in our backyard, looking for Harpers Ferry bottles. Dad usually had a leaf fire burning, so Marty could stay in the dump after dark, hunting by firelight. My father, keeping an eye on the fire, sat on the back step with this steel guitar, playing "Tie a Yellow Ribbon Around the Old Oak Tree," the only song he knew at first. That was before we had new neighbors on all sides of us and Dad was forced to plant bamboo along our fences to keep them all from seeing into our backyard.

Now he was playing the song again. It had been years, but it still sounded pretty good. He slid the metal bar up and down the steel strings, making the sound go high, then low.

I watched the music and good mood change everyone's faces. For a moment, they all seemed to forget why there were two park rangers in our house in the first place. Dad might have been the orneriest man on earth, but I had to wonder why he didn't let people in the house all the time.

In the corner, I glimpsed his precious 1858 Harpers Ferry breechloader, one of the first hundred of its type ever made, the one he enjoyed refusing good money for, lying on the floor, forgotten for the moment.

Ugley To Start With

* * *

We called her Skinny Minnie because she was terribly skinny when we first found her hung up in the chicken-wire fence across the street. At first, even Dad was nice to her, letting her stay inside, near the wood stove. Everybody wanted her on their bed, too, because her coat was soft and clean. She had obviously been an indoor cat, Mom said, wondering where she came from. Her small neck had no collar, but we checked at the houses on our street anyway. Nobody missed her.

When warm weather came that year, Skinny Minnie wanted to go outside. She sneaked out and stayed out for hours, sometimes overnight, and all the next day, too. I started finding her in the backyard, curled up in a sunny spot in the bamboo, sleeping. Soon she came and went as she pleased, and we learned not to expect her. Apparently, she had been an indoor/outdoor cat, as Mom called her.

One time, when Mom and I went for a walk down to the train station to see the river, we saw a silver tabby slinking around the old spur.

"Is that Skinny Minnie?" Mom asked. "Here, kitty-kitty."

It was Skinny Minnie all right, but she darted off. It amazed Mom that she had wandered so far from the house, and then didn't recognize any of us—ran from us like strangers.

When I got sick with shingles and was home in bed for a month, Skinny Minnie came to my bedroom window every afternoon. Somehow she was able to leap from the weedy lot next door to the sill of my stained-glass window, where she stood on the narrow ledge and meowed until I let her in. It was lonely in the afternoons, being sick and lying in bed for hours, my brothers in school, the sounds of the town far below, my mother far below, too, on the first floor, two flights down, where she couldn't always hear me when I cried out. Skinny Minnie was a welcome companion. She kneaded my stomach, but was too light to hurt the shingles on my side. I petted her until I fell asleep.

When I began to feel better, Mom brought me sketch paper and pencils. I sat up and started sketching. Every afternoon, Skinny Minnie lay like a donut on my bed, breathing in and out softly. She was still staying out all night and came in during the day just to sleep on my bed. When she did, I drew her as she slept. Every now and then, I reached over and petted her and admired how her coat felt. I looked at the silver stripes and blotches and tried to show them on paper by using the side of my pencil. I found that I could, without much trouble. Mom put one of the drawings in a frame.

With late spring came high weeds in the lot next door. Then the big bully cats arrived. You could see them swaggering through the new nettles, looking for trouble. My brother threw broken-up bricks at them every summer, but they came back every spring. They came from the Groves' house down near the church. Mrs. Grove had hair as red and frizzy as copper wire. She had no kids, and her cats and dogs were always dirty and on the loose. Her nephew Dink wandered through our backyard once and spit peanut butter on our swing set. My family might have been lowly West Virginians in the eyes of out-of-staters, but the Groves were really low-class. In the winter, when there were no weeds in the lot, you could see across into their back yard. There was a big pile of coal near their back porch, which was black from the coal being tracked in and out of the house.

Soon Skinny Minnie was getting into fights in the weedy lot. We could hear wild cat screams at night, and when she showed up at the door in the morning, her coat was dug open in places, and bloody sores glistened.

"Oh, poor thing," Mom said, stooping down to touch her.

She was in too much pain to be picked up and was in no mood to be touched, either. Mom tried to keep her on the back porch, in a box, until she healed, but she didn't take to it. Instead, she meowed at the door, wanting in. Dad said no, not until she healed.

Even after she healed, no one wanted her on their bed anymore and wouldn't let her sit on their lap, either, because of her scabs. I shoved her off mine because she was gross. We all did. Then, when she came in one day with more fresh wounds, Dad started chasing her out of the house for good.

"Get," he said whenever he saw her, and she shot out through a crack in the door.

Night after night, I heard her crying. A long, painful cry that wouldn't stop. I covered my ears with pillows, but still I could hear it. The Groves' fat cats were picking on her. I opened my window and shot my BB gun into the dark, trying to hit her or whatever was scaring her, to make the whole thing go away. But she kept crying, sometimes screaming out the most awful scream. I lay there praying she would die and go away and I would never remember her.

Sometimes whole days passed, and she didn't show up, and I forgot about her for a while. Then she came back, looking worse than ever. Her soft, perfect coat was matted with sticks and dried blood. She had a limp, too, and half an ear was missing. I couldn't bear to touch her, couldn't stand having her near me, either. All she did was sit there and moan, her wounds oozing. I pushed her away. She was gross. At night, she tried to get in through the stained-glass window, but I wouldn't open it. I could hear her faint meows. They seemed to go on for hours.

When summer came and I was home, I started shooting at Skinny Minnie with my BB gun whenever I saw her trying to come near the house. I could see the small, gold BB hit the side of her body. She jumped as if she had stepped on electricity and ran back into the overgrown lot. My body shuddered. If only she would die, then I wouldn't feel the embarrassment anymore. That's how my family was. Whatever it was, if it was ugly to start with, or turned ugly, we were ashamed of it and wanted it to go away.

Still, Skinny Minnie kept coming back, though more and more cautiously each time. A couple of times she looked up at me in the window from the edge of the weeds, as if asking why.

"Oh, poor thing, just look at her," Mom said whenever she found her at the door and Skinny Minnie held still for her. There were more raw sores everywhere. "Oh dear—Bill, what'd we do?"

Dad said nothing could be done.

I could feel my mother crying on the inside. She hated the way my father ran the house. Skinny Minnie was something else my father did wrong.

One day I realized that Skinny Minnie had not come back in a long time. I asked Mom where she went.

"Oh, I think the poor thing went away to die."

I just stared at her.

"They do that when they're sick," she said.

I did not wonder so much about death as where the place to die was. I checked the spot in the bamboo. I could still see the little impression her body left. I looked out my window into the weedy lot and called out. I went down to the train station and looked around the old spur.

It was just as well. I didn't want her around, unless her fur was perfect.

The Fence

***

It was early May and still raining. Dad had us on our new mountain property, all hunkered down in the lean-to, doing crummy little things. Not "property" the way normal people would see it, but woods full of milk jugs and rusted bean cans. He had the notion that we could clear the land—cut trails, build a cabin, pretend we had found paradise a kind of back-to-nature, Robinson Crusoe, *Foxfire* thing.

Andy, he had painting more No Trespassing signs and, me, he had separating washers from nuts and bolts rusted together. That was by far the crummiest task, but since I never listened and was always in trouble and couldn't work worth a lick anyway, I was lucky, Dad said, that there were nuts and bolts left rusted together in this world for me to separate. Otherwise, what good was I? Mom, he had keeping the bug fire. Greg, he had working out in the rain, restacking a pile of boards so that one sheet of plastic could cover it, instead of two. Since he got to wear a poncho that he thought made him look like Clint Eastwood, he didn't mind.

To my father, no task was ridiculous, if it meant saving something worth saving. And everything was worth saving. With a little figuring, Dad could repair or reuse anything. In the same spirit that he would wire-brush oily, burnt sparkplugs until they were shiny and clean, and then hold them out in his palms to admire like glossy metal sculptures, he would look at a rusted Chevy frame in the weeds as if you could build civilization on it. He saw materials in everything, and by his thinking, nothing in the world was being manufactured anymore, nothing being repaired, no new parts being sold. Civilization was falling, and he had the last salvage yard.

The lean-to was our last ditch. Having us huddled under it gave Dad the satisfaction of having beaten the elements with his own ingenuity. The lean-to was our kitchen, our dining room, and our living room, and he had built it with his own hands. The only reason we were dry on this day was his ability, his resourcefulness. And up here on the mountain, there was no one to question this ability, no neighbors to gawk at how tattered and filthy his lean-to was.

It was, in fact, a sturdy little structure made of a tight lattice of pine poles and thatch, with a black plastic cover that kept us dry and the wind off of us. One problem, however, was that smoke from the fire in the pit, located in front, continually drifted back inside the lean-to, eventually sending us out coughing. As a rule, you had to stay low to the ground just to breathe, but still the smoke stung your eyes. Another problem was that at its highest point, the lean-to was still too low to stand up in, so Mom, while tending the fire, constantly struggled with whether to stand bent over or just give in to an undignified position of getting on her knees on the hard ground. She ended up squatting in the dirt like an Indian woman, wood spiders all above her, though she didn't see them. They infested the underside of the thatched roof, and the smoke was driving them crazy.

Andy and I were well back under the opening, sitting cross-legged on pieces of burlap, our heads touching the angled roof. Smoke roiled back over us, but it was as if our lungs had grown filters, how we managed to sort air from smoke.

Around the sides of the lean-to hung lengths of wire used as hotdog sticks. Nothing else hung here, just these metal hotdog sticks, dozens of them, a whole line of them, like goods in an emporium. There were fancy ones with handles, others with forks for roasting two, even three dogs at once. There was a grand one that could hold half a dozen dogs, and there was an unusual one with a long, curved handle for reaching around the fire to the best cooking coals. Dad had made them all out of fence wire that he had picked up in industrial-size reels somewhere on the mail route. It was plain wire, without barbs, coated with some chemical that had to be burned off over the flames before we could use the wire to cook with. It irked our mother that Dad had half a dozen reels of good wire, but no inclination to replace the rusted fences around our property. For him, hot dog sticks were a fun art. Wire art. All he needed was the wire and a pair of needle-nosed pliers.

Outside, the rain, caught in a gust, picked up for a moment and sounded like a shower.

"William, I don't think it's letting up any," Mom said for the second time this afternoon, waving smoke out of her face. Long past was her subtle suggestion that this was not a good day to try to get any work done, and long past as well was his answer that he could always find something to do.

Something to do. I hated his way of looking at us, as if all we were, were bad kids to put to work. He was standing outside, under a tree that had enough leaves to keep the rain off, sawing up clapboards in foot-long lengths for Andy to paint white. The boards came from an old house that had been torn down recently. Another of his treasures.

I sat back under the lean-to, thinking about kids from school who were inside their nice dry homes this afternoon. The rain had been coming down for hours, and the hard dirt road that ran down through out property was melting to one side, like soaked clay spun hard on a potter's wheel. Jezebel, our mule, stood over in the rain, her coat flattened. I could see her breath in the cold, damp air. The drizzle, you could just tell, would go on all day.

I would do anything to see my friend, Deedee. I hadn't seen her forever, it seemed, and whenever I called, her mother said she still had the flu. I looked over at Andy. He was tuning us all out by listening to the Bullets game on a small transistor radio he had cleverly taped to the side of his cap. Dad let him listen since both of his hands were still free to work and since he was keeping the noise low. I think it was also because he was ingenious that Dad let him listen. Andy was showing that handyman inclination, not to mention being extra productive, by painting so many clapboards that they ran around the inside of the lean-to like a picket fence. I was jealous. Andy had found his little escape.

I looked out through the smoke. The rain was hitting every leaf on the mountain, and they dripped down by the thousands. As far as I could see, nothing but wet leaves and gray sky cluttered up with rusted junk. I couldn't take this all day. I wouldn't last. The back of my neck was cold, and my hands were streaked with orange rust water from the bottom of the coffee can filled with nuts and bolts. But this said nothing of what was going on inside me. I had to ask, and I would beg if I had to.

"Mom, can I go see Deedee?"

There were many things not to ask in my family. In fact, most questions were better off not asking. We were a "No, you can't" family. Some questions were so unspeakable that if asked, they took form like a bottomless hole between my parents. This was one. They both looked up as if they had just seen the entirety of my life, and for the first time they agreed on something—the view was not promising.

Dad stopped sawing and looked in the lean-to. "No, I told you *no*."

"Well, now William, wait a minute," my mother said back—there was fear in her voice, fear for me, but there was also objection, last-ditch objection. My father was saying no to the only thing that mattered to me, and ordinarily, if he had been denying Greg or Andy something, my mother would have gone along with it. But I was her favorite. I knew that full well. I was growing up hearing that from my brothers as if they were telling me I was adopted. I did not really wonder why she was protecting me—I just relied on it.

"Wait a minute, hell," he said back. When it came to my father, hell was like a fly that wouldn't leave him alone.

Andy stopped brushing the board and looked up, and Greg stared over. He knew as well as I did that affection was like a sin in my Catholic family, never to be shown or spoken of. My parents were afraid of the very sight of it. The only time Dad showed Mom affection was when she discovered an azalea bush for him not to accidentally cut down, and then it was in the form of letting her use his new hand pruners, and the only way she knew to be affectionate back was not to serve his Hamburger Helper dried out.

"William," my mother said again, this time in a pleading voice, "she's his friend."

My father looked into the lean-to at her as if she were the hardest woman in the world to put up with. "I can't help that," he said.

He meant just that. He couldn't help that I was alive and causing problems. I wasn't *his* fault. If she had listened to him, they would have never had me. I had heard this before.

"Well, that doesn't make any sense," she said right back, as outraged by him as he was by her.

"Damn it, Katie," he said, pulling the tree saw out of the log and pointing it at her like a gun, "that girl is not right—and we don't need to be having this conversation right now."

I was afraid for my mother, afraid because she was getting herself in trouble, arguing with him.

"You can't expect him not to have any friends," she said.

"Let him have his damn friends in school," he said back. "This place is for working!" He pointed his saw at the ground. If it had been a digging iron, he would have driven it into the soil.

I didn't expect her to win this fight for me, but I felt better just having it out in the open. Now they knew. Andy. Greg. They all knew that Dad was keeping me from seeing Deedee.

"I just don't understand," she said again, but this time in a voice of defeat that kept him from raising his more.

"You don't have to," he said, pushing her nose in it.

I gave him my ugliest face and blurted out, "You get to see Mrs. Jackson!" As hard as I shouted, I was still sitting way back in the lean-to, and with all the smoke around me and the slanted ceiling hanging low and the plastic lining on either side, my voice was louder to myself than to anyone else.

My mother's head came up with a snap. "William, what's he talking about?" she said.

The whole world was looking at my father. As God is my witness, he had been sneaking over to see Deedee's mother. I knew because sometimes I saw him in the woods heading over there as I was sneaking back. I didn't know if he and Deedee's mother were just friends, but Mrs. Jackson was still a woman, and so was my mother.

Accused, Dad began a guilty smile. I rarely saw this face. Once, when a Charles Town policeman stopped him for having a taillight out. Dad tried to use his personality routine on him and it didn't work. Another time, when he and Mom had an argument and Grandma came to the door. It was as if his face, in smiling, was dripping off him, like melting wax, so that all the sternness was running down, and left was the bony skull of a timid, fearful boy.

Guilt was visible only for an instant. Back was his grim, ox-blood face. He pointed the tree saw in the direction of the Jackson's house. "Katie, he's been goin' over there every chance he gets. He's not to bother them, you hear me?"

Mom's face was creased up, puzzled now by more than my accusation. "I'm sure he's no bother, William, not to their daughter," she said back. It was Grandma's voice she used again, a voice that brought to mind a deep, still lake that, even when the worst autumn wind blew, showed only a few ripples. "If she invited him and it's all right with her mother—"

My old man hit his chest several times to show that he was head of this family. He hit it so hard his voice rattled like weights in a clock. "It's not all right! It's not all right with me!"

This was how he won, by acting like an ape. Mom looked at him as if he were completely crazy. None of the men on her side of the family ever behaved this way. This was pure, uncalled-for, Irish disgrace. Then she slowly turned to me and, in the voice of surrender, said, "Jason, you can always see her in school."

I was already halfway crying and it didn't take long for me to make a real scene of it. It was my only comfort, my only recourse, too, for once I started crying, I found my place in the family again. Crying reminded me that I was the youngest and would always be the youngest. Crying was something I better get used to. Besides, I really was losing my insides. All that Deedee was to me was aching. Mom might have thought of it as a crush or puppy love, but I knew it was the feeling of a lifetime.

"I love her, Mom!" I cried.

Dad, stepping back, got a kink in his face—a twisted-up, embarrassed smile. I never hated him so much as I did at that moment. He was so embarrassed by my feelings that he had to look that way, as if I had become utterly ridiculous.

"Oh, shit, he loves her," he said, looking up, as if God had never given out such a difficult son.

Love, you see, was a word we didn't say in our family. God *loved* us. That was okay to hear, as long as Father Zimmer, not Father "Ron," said it. Love was a fine word for Valentine's Day, too, and even for letters home from men in the service. Our cousin Derrick wrote "Love, Derrick" in his letters from Japan. But other than that, love was like chicken with too much ginger. Dad never said he loved Mom, never uttered the word. Damn, hell, shit—he said these as often as conjunctions. But love? He didn't love anyone or anything. Not the peacefulness of the woods. Not even his guns. Those he cherished.

I loved Deedee. Mom looked at us in concern. Andy just looked scared.

"William," my mother said, shoving sticks around in the fire, "as far as I'm concerned, you started all this." She shoved a thick stick deep into the fire, causing a plume of sparks to rise up against the underside of the lean-to. "How can you expect him not to be interested? His own father is!"

Greg threw a board down hard on the pile, and the sound of it clapped through the damp air. "Stop it, you all!" he yelled over.

Dad looked back at him. "Oh now look. See what he's started," he said, meaning me. He turned to blame me for Greg's outburst, but Andy caught his eye first, and Dad yelled at him for dripping paint. Hell was everywhere again, buzzing around my father like a bee.

Mom went on looking hurt, and my father, when he finished yelling at Andy, sounded tired of fighting with all of us. "Katie, why are you acting this way?" he asked. He was practically begging her to let up.

"Well, William, I've never even seen their house," she said, in a voice that seemed as coiled as a bedspring. "Doesn't that strike you as strange?"

"Oh, shit," he snapped back. "They live over there somewhere. You act like it's a secret."

Mom was looking right at him. "Just 'over there somewhere'?"

Greg chimed in from a distance. "I know where it is," he said to Mom.

Andy piped up, too. "It's that road that goes past Hank's," he told her.

"Mom, she's been sick all week," I said. "She needs me."

"Well, I'd just like to see this house for myself," Mom said, rising off the dirty cold ground and brushing off her pants. This voice was her own. Not Grandma's, but her own, resulting from everything he had done wrong with the family and from what she could keep from happening again.

Dad went wimpy. "Oh, damn it, Katie, it's raining. Now sit back down. You're acting crazy."

"I'll show you where it is, Mom," Greg said, pulling off the hood of his poncho, meaning business.

Dad spun around. "No you won't. Get back to work, Mister."

While Dad was growling at Greg, Mom turned to me and asked, in a voice that no one else seemed to hear, where the path was from our property to the Jacksons' house.

"Damn it, Katie," my father went on ranting, "there's must be half a dozen houses over there. You act like it's a big secret."

"I'll show you, Mom," Greg said again.

My father spun around again, and Greg backed off.

Mom pulled her stocking cap down over her ears. "Don't you talk to me about secrets," she said. She stepped out in the drizzle and started up the road. Greg headed after her. Andy shot through the smoke of the lean-to, and I right behind him.

"Oh, all right," Dad said, pulling the saw out of the clapboard and resting it against the dry trunk of the big tree he was working under. And just like that, my father had lost control of his pygmies. And his fire keeper.

Greg had taken over, as far as protective sons went, being just a step behind Mom. Andy was behind Greg, protecting him, and I followed behind Andy. Dad soon caught up, but remained half a step behind Mom the whole way up the muddy road to the south end.

My family was on a little adventure, with Mom's curiosity and determination leading the way. She stopped long enough for me to show her where to cross the fence at the south end. This in itself was ridiculous. Old Rusty had put the wire fence in God knows how long ago, and anyone could see that it was now nothing more than rusted, crumbly wire, knee-high in the leaves, entangled in itself and falling down and, if not falling down, low enough to step over in any place without any guidance from my father.

Still, he was upset on this occasion that it lay crumpled to the ground. Naturally he blamed me for knocking it down, ruining it, during my many sneaky trips over to the Jacksons', he said. He never looked more pathetic than when we all marched over the fence, and he was on his hands and knees in the wet leaves, trying to mend it. I turned around to see him left behind by all of us.

Mom was meanwhile making her own trail through the woods. Only the biggest trees dared to stand in her way. Greg was following her closely, then Andy.

I noticed them right away—black-and-orange, plastic, store-bought No Trespassing signs nailed to the trees. They had not been here before, but there were plenty of them now, everywhere so that we could see them, so that we *must* see them.

I saw something else up head that looked different—flashes of white, one, two, three, and more, upright like short, branchless trees. New fence posts spaced evenly across the woods. Shiny new strands of barbed wire stretched across them.

Mom stopped a few feet from this new fence and stood waiting for my father. Greg and Andy were milling around behind her, not yet understanding.

"What the hell is this?" my father said, catching up with us at the new fence and stopping, purely by chance, beside me. It seemed a big, strange moment, the two of us standing side-by-side, looking at this new fence. My father turned to me and, in a voice I didn't recognize, asked, "Did you know about this?"

I shook my head, but I knew what it meant. It had Mr. Jackson all over it, and the message was clear—my father and I were *both* not welcome.

Dad knew, too, in his heart. You would think the fence was electrified the way he kept his distance from it.

Mom, who stood closest to it, turned around, and, looking confused, asked, "William, is this new?"

Of course it was new, he said, grouchy with her. Couldn't she see the new posts, the freshly turned dirt, and the shiny strands of wire?

Mom looked back at the fence as if it were some great riddle and asked, "Did *she* have it put up?"

"Katie, I don't know," my father said, as if these were the last words he would ever say.

Greg and Andy were spinning their heads between my father and my mother, looking confused themselves.

Mom was still looking back at Dad when she asked, "Should we go on?"

He was staring far away, so far away that he seemed to look around the world and back at himself. "No," he said.

I had never felt we were a family before, but at that moment, we were all on the same side of this new fence—and all together, in not being wanted beyond this fence.

Mom gave the fence another look and laughed. It was that loopy girlish sound she made, that corkscrew into his shoulder. She wasn't blind anymore. "Well, William," she said, "it wasn't *all* your son this time."

Greg and Andy, having walked up to the fence, were touching the new wire. Andy put his fingers on shiny sharp barbs. None of us had seen a brand-new barbed wire before. They pulled on the strands to test their tautness. They were like guitar strings, Greg said.

Admiration of the fence insulted Dad even more. He turned and started back. Greg couldn't wait to kick a post, to show his contempt. And since the fence post shifted a little when he did kick it, he called out to Dad that it wasn't put very far into the ground and that he could knock it over easily. He looked at Dad, waiting for his approval to push it over. But Dad was walking on.

As we all walked back, with Dad in the lead now, I heard Mom ask him, "Did she say anything about it?" There was sympathy in her voice.

But my father remained irritable and embarrassed—wounded.

"I think we should tear it down," Greg said to make him feel better.

Andy was listening to the game again and now at a higher volume, since the roar was out of our father.

I felt sorry for Dad. He wasn't wanted anymore. Mr. Jackson was putting his foot down. Part of me was glad. If I couldn't see Deedee, then he couldn't see her mother.

We Never
Liked Them Anyway

* * *

Mom and I had heard the weather report first thing. The storm
had dumped more than a foot on the eastern panhandle overnight,
closing schools in Morgan, Berkeley, and Jefferson counties. I tore
off for the closet for my galoshes while "Bob in the Morning" went
on with the county news:

"The Leetown Fish Hatchery has announced plans to expand its
Jefferson County facility . . ."

Mom went on ironing, her body doing a little shimmy as she
worked the iron back and forth.

"Jason, keep your boots snapped up today," she called out. "Remember what happened the last time?"

Mom was still pressing my flannel shirt when I hurried back
with my boots on. Every time she set the iron down, it hissed.
When she picked it up again, it gurgled.

"In other local news, Harpers Ferry National Park Superintendent Ronald Wilkinson faces sexual harassment charges by two
Park employees. In an internal investigation, the employees alleged
that Wilkinson used sexually offensive remarks repeatedly over the

last several years. Local businessman Lee Jackson, outspoken . . ."

The old iron hissed like a serpent, covering up the next few words. Mom's face, in the steam, looked as hard as copper.

". . . calling for his resignation. An investigation by the EEOC is scheduled for next month. In other news . . ."

She put the iron down. I could see every one of her forty-seven years whittled out to the end of her nose.

"There must be some mistake," she said. She looked at me. "Did he just say Ronald Wilkinson? He did, didn't he? My God."

Just then, "Bob in the Morning" started laughing his hyena laugh. His timing was terrible. Mom walked out of the room. In the kitchen, she put her hands on the table as if it was all she could do to hold herself up. When I came in, she was sitting down, pretending to look at a postcard.

She looked up. "Our Ronald Wilkinson?"

My mother loved him the first time she saw him. It was a winter morning three years ago, and she was on the front porch, feeding our dog. She looked up, and, jogging down the street in the snow was a man in red long johns! Smoking a cigar at the same time! He had wild copper hair and a smiling rugged face and a big sturdy body bouncing around. In a hearty voice, he called out hello to her—hello by name—"Morning, Mrs. Stevens." As Mom stood there gaping, he gave her a second wave with his cigar hand. The look was on her face for hours. *That* was our new Park superintendent? *That* was Ronald Wilkinson?

Not once in the thirty years that the National Park Service had been in Harpers Ferry had a superintendent ever said hello to my mother, much less made a spectacle of himself in the street. Our last superintendent was Marvin W. Phillips III from Annapolis, Maryland. What a perfect snot he was. He had a chalk-white daughter no one liked either. He lived in a big house on the hill and came out only to whisk around town in his sprawling new car. He waved to no local, certainly not to *my mother.*

Mom stood and finished ironing my shirt.

"Have you heard anything, Jason?" she asked, her voice soft and strange.

When I shook my head, she looked off. At the same time, Bob's hyena laugh came back on. She set the iron down, marched over to the radio, and turned it off with such force she twisted the knob clean off. When she tried to stick it back on, I could see the bones in her face coming out.

Shocking! Filthy! She would never listen to that station again.

I stood there behind her.

"Oh those poor boys," she said, looking off into space as if seeing into their home, seeing Mrs. Wilkinson, Mr. Wilkinson. Then she turned to me, bent down, and said, "Whatever you do today, Jason, keep those poor boys away from the radio."

Keeping Mike and Adam away from a radio was easy. We were never indoors anyway. We had a whole national park to play in. Down at The Point, it turned into a game of chase. As I led them across the train bridge into Maryland, in my mind, I was taking them out of distance of WXVA, which I imagined stopped at the state line, at some great invisible wall. At the ruins of the Salty Dog bar, which had been painted white by the park and looked almost invisible in the snow, I started climbing up the mountain.

In the light snow, I could see a million white flakes falling over the train tunnel, a perfect dark hole in the mountain. I pulled myself up from tree to tree, the wet snow peppering my face, and worked my way around outcroppings, not stopping to look down. Soon I was in the mist and fog and light snow where eagles and hawks rode the currents up and down like elevators. Mike and Adam's shouts were faint and far below.

When I reached the main face, I ran out of trees and jagged rocks to hold on to. That was always the problem. No one ever made it beyond this point in the winter. Not only did I come to a stop, but with nothing under the elbow-deep snow to pinch onto, it took all my strength just to hold on. Still, I could feel the earth pulling me outward. I imagined Mom coming out on the front porch to feed our dog, looking up, and seeing through all the snow and fog across the river the little blue X that I was on the cliffs. And I wasn't even half the distance up Stevie had gone before he fell.

Stevie, my first cousin, died when he fell off Chimney Rock above me, where nobody climbed, anytime of the year. He lay in the ravine below most of the day before a man found him. Some people said he died from the fall. Others said it was because he lay there for so long. Mom said it didn't really matter which. No one could understand why he had tried to climb it alone.

Mike yelled up from a ledge some fifty feet below, telling me to come back down. Below him, about the same distance, was Adam, and below him, still all the way down on the road, was Ron Ron, their retarded brother.

I had one chance. I swung myself to the side, slipped hard against the rock face, and dropped about ten feet, landing on my butt in an outcropping of deep snow. My old, snap-up galoshes popped open and instantly filled with snow. If these cliffs over the tunnel at Harpers Ferry had been Mt. Rushmore, I would have just landed on Lincoln's nose.

Mike and Adam climbed up about the same time.

"Man, J," said Mike, picking me up out of the snow, "what's wrong with you today?"

"Nothing."

"Something is," said Adam, grinning. He was standing back and had his devil face on as usual. He wanted to see me break my neck, but that didn't mean we weren't friends.

I looked closely at the two of them, searching for any sign that they knew about the radio report, about their father's awful situation. Mike said we should head back down. For that, Adam called me a pud. That was how it always worked between the three of us. The nicer Mike was to me, the meaner Adam got.

I started climbing sideways, pulling myself over tree by tree. Mike shouted down to the road to tell Ron Ron to meet us on the fire truck road. The snow on the side of the mountain was knee-deep, so by the time we reached the fire truck road, my jeans were wet all the way up and the insides of my galoshes were clamping my feet in hard slush. In the road, where the snow wasn't so deep, Mike and Adam saw my busted open boots and wet jeans. They were both wearing snowsuits and high zip-up boots. Mike looked worried, Adam happy.

I took off running up the fire truck road for the cabin at the top. Soon the snow was so deep I had to knee my way through. Adam, excited about seeing me freeze to death, was keeping up. Mike yelled out that it wasn't funny anymore. Ron Ron was just making his way up the far turn.

The woods back here were quiet and undisturbed. There were birds on the snow-filled limbs, and cold sunlight came down in rays like in a painting. As I ran, I thought about what Mom had said—*keep them away from the radio*. I was taking them about as far away from the radios in town as anyone could. I also thought about what we had heard. Sexual harassment? It seemed a strange accusation, as if the words didn't say what was really meant. There was flirting, which everybody did, and there was rape, which nobody did. This was something in between that nobody knew exactly what it was. I had seen most of the women who worked for the park. It must have been the blonde one who always wore a tight green skirt. All the rangers looked at her. I tried to imagine Mr. Wilkinson saying something wrong to her. I couldn't—he was married and had a good family.

On the steep incline over the creek, I fell face-first in the snow, twice. The second time, I hit my chin against my knee. By the time I hauled myself into the cabin, I could hardly feel my feet anymore. When I stomped around on the floor, it felt like I had peg legs. Outside, Mike was calling out, his shouts muffled by the heavy snow hanging down. His big shadow came through the door and across the bare cabin floor.

"Damn, J," he said, seeing me shivering over by the cold fireplace, "what's wrong with you today?"

"Nothin'."

"Don't say nothin'."

He gave me a concerned look. He knew I was growing up with a mother who made me into a sissy and a father who was never around.

Adam came in behind him, panting and grinning. He had never seen anyone near dead before. Ron Ron came in next. Snot was running down his nose. The three of them stood looking at me, their breaths coming out as white as fog.

"His crazy father's come back," Adam said.

My father was crazy all right. Everybody knew that. Ever since Mom threw him out of the house last year over Mrs. Jackson, he had been living on his mountain property. Soon after, he got suspended from his job at the post office because of his drinking. He was never coming back, or at least I hoped he was gone for good. But like everything else in the rotten West Virginia woods, his ugliness would probably creep back into our lives.

I kept stomping my feet on the floor, trying to get blood back into them. Adam was looking at me with a snarl to his upper lip. He hated how weak I was. It drove him crazy that I could be like a girl and stand myself. He whipped out his bowie knife.

"Hold 'em!" he said. "Need to amputate the feet off a damn local!"

He was imitating somebody crazy when he did this voice. John Brown? Maybe his father, since Mr. Wilkinson had a raspy voice. It always made Mike laugh, and that was all the encouragement Adam ever needed.

Ron Ron grabbed me by the shoulders like a battery-powered Frankenstein using just enough force, and Adam pressed the shiny blade against my leg. I knew he was pretending because Mike was still grinning. As long as Mike wasn't concerned, neither was I.

The first time I saw Mike I loved him the way my mother loved his father. From my window, I had been watching him run the Stone Steps near the church. There were sixty-eight steps from bottom to top. He ran them half a dozen times without stopping. Then he came into our backyard, gulped from our water hose for the longest while, and let out a belch that came clear through the three-foot stone walls of our house. My mother looked around and said, "What was that?" Later, he came to our door and said he needed me as weight on his back. He was going to carry a 110-pound barbell—the whole Montgomery Ward weight set—up and down the Stone Steps, and he needed extra weight to make it a challenge. All the way up and down, as I clung to his sweaty back and he stumbled over the steps and tourists gawked and pointed, he burst out laughing at how crazy we must have looked. I thought that was the coolest, how he could work so hard at something but take it lightly, too. Even while he was wheezing like a horse, nearly dying, it was funny to him how he appeared to others. I had never seen that in a person.

I had also never seen a father and son like Mike and Mr. Wilkinson. After karate class on Tuesday nights, they usually sat together in a ranger jeep, waiting for Adam. They were the same size in the shoulders and the same height even when sitting down. As they talked in low voices, they looked like big friends. They reminded me of the profiles on Mount Rushmore; even when they were looking off at different angles, they seemed to fit together.

Adam, meanwhile, was pressing the knife harder against my leg, daring me to take it. The last time he got carried away like this, he jabbed me in the hand with a pencil and said it was an accident. Then he stabbed me in other hand and said that was an accident, too. Thanks to him, I had matching black dots on my palms from where pencil lead had broken off under the skin. A girl in my class said I looked like Christ.

When he turned the blade point against my leg, it cut in—I flung my arms and cried out until Ron Ron let me go. Rubbing my leg, I looked over at Mike. With his psycho brother around, he never stuck up for me. But when just the two of us camped out in this cabin, he didn't stand over in the corner, embarrassed of me. It was our little house then. We arranged the metal cots in front of the fireplace, brought in firewood from outside, and sat around eating Doritos and bouncing on the cots until we got bored enough to hike down to the cliffs and pretend to be Civil War soldiers shooting at the town.

Adam flung the knife at the wall, sticking it in.

"Damn locals," he said in his John Brown voice. "They lie!"

I looked over. "Lie about what?" I turned to Mike. Suddenly he was glaring at me as if things between us had changed long before today. They knew about their father after all.

"Ron Ron," said Adam, "say, 'Jason's cousin fell off a cliff.'"

Ron Ron said it back in his weird, fast drone, and Adam burst out laughing.

"And now he's nothing but a big red stiff."

"Nothing but red stiff."

"Lie about what?" I asked again.

Mike wouldn't even look at me.

"Why don't you toughen up, Jason?" he said, pretending to search for kindling in the corners of the cabin.

"Why don't you get a life?" I shot back.

It was not what I wanted to say. Adam was egging us on just by being here. Mike found a burnt stick and kicked it into the center of the floor.

"Your mother should have remarried," he said in all seriousness.

"Well, your father shouldn't run around in his underwear."

Adam was excited. Mike and me arguing?

"He thinks you're his dead cousin," he laughed to his brother.

The worst feelings swarmed in me as I looked at Mike for a truce.

"Damn, don't cry about it," he said.

"I'm not crying."

"Crying, lying local," Adam laughed. "It's because of his mom. She babies him."

My head whipped up in anger, and I lashed out.

"I heard about your father."

I kept my eyes on Mike. It was between him and me. A shiny, embarrassed smile broke over his face. For a second, he actually looked scared of me.

"That sexual harassment thing," I said just as smugly as I could.

Adam was too scared to know what to do, and Mike was just standing there, not so proud anymore. The great Mike ashamed. It was exciting bringing Mr. Decathlon down to size.

"Ron Ron," I said, "say, 'Dad with a stiff one.'"

"Dad with a stiff one," stupid Ron Ron said.

Adam, switching sides, burst out laughing, and Mike didn't know which of us to tell to shut up. The great Mike taken down a peg. For the first time, I had leverage. If I couldn't have a good father, neither could he.

He turned and shoved his brother for starting it all, sending him down in the snow dragged in on the floor. In the scuffle, Adam ended up near me, and when Mike came at both of us, Adam and I were out the door, running up the fire truck road together. It felt great to actually be on his side for once.

All the kids called him a psycho because he was always doing crazy stunts, like running his sled into gravestones. He was also a bully and a rat. The first time I hung around him he busted me in the mouth in a game of a touch football. As I ran home to Mom, trying to hold back the tears, Mike came along to make sure I'd be all right. Adam tagged along for just the opposite reason—to see me cry. Whenever I glanced at him, he had this excitement on his face, as if seeing me crying was the best thrill in the world, better than the dead body he supposedly saw in the back of the funeral home.

Mike, as it turned out, wasn't chasing us, so at the top of the hill, Adam and I slowed down. His crazy grin was wearing off, and he started looking uncomfortable. He never liked being alone with me, and he seemed to be remembering that now. I was too much like a girl for him, the way I talked about feelings all the time.

When we came to where the road forked off to the Blue-blazed Trail, he looked back to see if his brother was following. My feet weren't cold anymore, I told him. Not that he cared. If I loved Mike because he reminded me of my cousin, then I hated Adam because he was like an old abused police dog you couldn't trust. The trick was to act friendly, then work behind his back.

"When my dad cheated on my mom," I said, "she was crazy for days."

I thought he would tell me to shut up, but he glanced over, looking worried. He had this scared look that made his face skinny.

"She move in with your grandma?"

I nodded. Adam knew my grandmother. She was the woman always telling him not to run over her flowers.

"You think your father's gonna be transferred?"

It was either hit me or answer me. He had lost his edge, and I had gained mine. I knew what he was afraid of. When he first came to Harpers Ferry, he was small for his age like me. That was another reason he did crazy stunts all the time, to make himself stand out. If his father was transferred, he'd have to start over in another town, and chances were, another town would be nothing like Harpers Ferry. There'd be no cliffs for him to hang from, no rivers to act like Tom Sawyer in, no tunnels to let a train chase him out of. He'd have no way to stand out.

When he shrugged, I said, "Yeah, moving would suck."

Mike could read my tricks, but Adam was a dummy. A dummy with people and a dummy in school. In the hall, he would flip his textbooks over to hide the covers so that no one knew he was in phase three, for below average students. He was so afraid Ron Ron's retarded brain was in him, especially because he looked so much like him.

I started jogging, making him follow me for once.

"Yeah, my mom's all worried about your mom," I said.

His mother, it was well enough known, had a mild heart condition. I wanted to remind Adam of that. He stopped again and looked back for his brother.

"He'll catch up," I said. "Come on."

At the top of the mountain where the trees thinned and the snow had drifted, we reached a level stretch on the trail.

"I wonder why they call it harassment," I said, slowing down.

Adam grabbed girls in school all the time. He and his gang did. Sometimes they took it too far, pinching and grabbing from all sides, all of his buddies at once.

"Remember Trudy Grove?" I laughed.

He always gave it hard to Trudy. He thought nothing of grabbing her right between the legs and fingering around for a good long second.

"Remember Marianne Childs?" I said.

Supposedly he had sex with Marianne in her pool. When she and her parents left for vacation the next day, he brought everybody by for a look at his "gysum" he said was still floating in the pool. I thought it was soap scum.

We came to a tree across the trail. Adam sat down on it and looked down at his shiny boots in the snow.

"Peg Wilt," he said in a weak little voice I hadn't heard in years. "She called the house." He reached down, picked up a stick, and winged it into the trees. "Mom went crazy."

"Peg Wilt?" I said. "Piggy Peg Wilt?"

He looked up at me. I was grinning. Peg Wilt was nothing but a local. She had one of those GS-7 administrative jobs that didn't pay well and that the park gave to local women out of pity. Mr. Wilkinson and a local woman? I couldn't wait to tell Mom.

"Man, Peg Wilt," I kept saying, grinning and shaking my head as if there was no tomorrow for his family. If Peg Wilt was one of the two park women, then the other one was probably a local, too.

"Did your mom catch him with her?"

I wasn't scared of him anymore. He was like something wounded and on a chain, too. He looked over, too dumb to figure out I was making everything worse.

"They're talking about jail time," I said.

He looked up. "Who?"

"The guy on the radio."

He got an angry look, as if going to beat up the guy on the radio. I snickered inside as I walked around behind him, seeing how small and slump-shouldered he looked. He started saying that he didn't want to move, that his father had messed everything up. He was pathetic, Mr. Tough Guy suddenly talking like me, after picking on me all these years.

I picked up a clump of snow that had a stone in it and threw it at the side of his face as hard as I could. It exploded against his face, and he went reeling off the log. But he bounced up as quickly, all wild-eyed, ready to kill. I pretended to be scared, and then pretended it was an accident, saying I was aiming for his shoulder. He stood ready to punch me, but instead flung off his glove and touched the side of his face. When he saw blood on his fingertips, he was more angry, and more scared. Seeing him weak and helpless was the best feeling.

"It's just a scratch," I said. But it wasn't. It was a good deep cut.

He looked around for Mike, his face all scrunched up, looking like his retard brother. I glanced down at the knife at his waist and thought about jumping him and sticking him with it. But I went on acting sorry and looking afraid, and that overwhelmed his stupid little mind and made him stand there, not sure what to feel or do. All I had to do now was stick to my lie that it was an accident.

As we headed back down to the cabin, I ran alongside him just to see if he would cry. Whenever he glanced over at me, I let him see the excitement on my face, as if seeing him crying was the best thrill in the world.

When we reached the fire truck road, Mike was coming up the hill—limping! Adam yelled out, asking what happened, and Mike said he had twisted his ankle when we tripped him in the cabin. With each step, his big frame fell to one side. The great and powerful Mike limping. It was like the end of something.

He hobbled up to us, saw Adam's blood-streaked cheek, and looked at me. I knew at that moment I was no good at being mean. Everything was backward. I hadn't meant to bring up his father. It was Adam. He wouldn't stop bothering me.

"It was an accident," I said.

He said nothing to me, but instead told Adam to wipe the blood off his face. While Adam bent down and started wiping with snow, Mike stood with his back to me. All I could do now was give him a chance to get back at me and hope he took it.

"Remember Mrs. Jackson?" I said. "My father cheated on my mom with her."

He looked at me, shook his head as if I was just a stupid little kid, and started limping down the road. Adam, his face wet from snow, was laughing at me again, back on the winning side. Following them, I thought of the worst things to say about my father.

"He used to hide brandy in his desk. That's how he got suspended."

I ran up to Mike and said I didn't believe a word of what was said on the radio. My mother didn't either. No one would. He gave me a flash of anger. Why did I keep talking about it?

I was all but crying. I wanted him to be sad for once. Why did he have to be so strong? I was tired of always getting the pity. What was wrong with wanting to give it for a change? Why couldn't he put down his father, too?

Adam's eyebrows were up as if I had just ruined myself a thousand times and not even he could enjoy this anymore. Mike just turned and limped on. I tried to egg on his anger.

"I know it's Piggy Peg Wilt."

He stopped.

"At least Mrs. Jackson wasn't a *local*," I said, trying to laugh about it.

He turned and limped back to me. I hoped he was going to punch me in the face, but in the calmest voice, all he said was, "What would your mom think, Jason?"

Adam laughed again.

"Jason's cous fell off the cliff," I started yelling to make fun of myself, "and now he's nothing but a big red stiff."

On the turn down to the cabin, Mike started limping bad. I watched as he climbed up on his brother's back. I had never seen Mike needing anyone before. Adam, stumbling to one side, strained to hold him. As I followed in his deep, dragged out tracks, I couldn't take my eyes off the two of them hooked together, Mike's bad ankle dangling, Adam's legs wobbling to carry them both. It was more than piggyback I was seeing. It was brothers.

Halfway down to the cabin, Mike fell off, but in the tumble, he and Adam laughed the same hearty laugh they were known for, a laugh that said nothing fazed them, not a cut face or a twisted ankle, not something on the radio. Even in the worst moments there was something funny.

We found Ron Ron down near the cabin, standing under a tree, mumbling to himself. He wasn't violent like Adam, though he sure looked it, with his scrunched-up face and way of standing in one spot forever, twisting his hair up into a crown of thorny curls, saying weird half-dirty words over and over, like "dick suck" and "butt fart." He sure spooked the tourists in town. Mike looked down at my old galoshes and asked if my feet were still cold. When I acted huffy and didn't answer, he told Ron Ron to carry me.

Ron Ron came forward like Frankenstein obeying orders and bent down. But I didn't want to put my legs and arms around a retard. I wanted Mike. I had already said I was sorry. What else could I do?

The four of us headed through the snow, Mike riding piggy-back on Adam, then Ron Ron, then, about twenty yards behind, me. All the way down the mountain I had to listen to Ron Ron drone, "Jason sad, Jason weak, Jason crying," while Adam went on laughing his heart out.

When I got home, Mom still had the radio on. It had been on all day, and she hadn't been able to turn it off. The same news about Mr. Wilkinson was on every hour, over and over. She seemed sick of hearing it, but at the same time kept hoping to hear more. School would probably be open tomorrow.

One look at me and she knew something was wrong. I told her it was Peg Wilt, and she looked at me as if another shop full of precious old antiques had burned down.

"Peg Wilt?" she said. "Are you sure?"

I nodded with all the bitterness the day had given me. "They told me."

She looked off into space, back into the same room then glanced back at me. "They told you? Oh, Jason, what have you boys been talking about today?"

I made it as bad as I could. I said Mr. Wilkinson fooled around on Mrs. Wilkinson all the time. "He's always been that way."

Mom looked at me as if whatever I had heard today, I had heard too much.

"And they just talked about it with you?"

I nodded the biggest lie of my life.

Mom never talked to me about Mrs. Jackson. Instead, I had to listen to her and Dad fighting over her, especially to Mom's hysterical voice cutting through the floor at night like a corkscrew drill. When Dad moved out, Mom went to see Father Ron, but I had no one to talk to about it. I wanted her to feel guilty about that now.

All evening I watched her looking at that space directly in front of her where she put everything she worried about.

"Well, I guess it's true," she finally said, "if they say so."

I told her that Adam had tried to start a fight with me over it.

"What about Mike?" she said. "He's still your friend, isn't he?"

I said nothing, and that only upset her further.

The Wallet

* * *

During breakfast our dog started barking. Then there was a rap on the door. Mom, Melinda, and I looked at one another. Mom, wiping her hands on her apron, stood and went to the blinds. It was Skip Howell from her office, she said. She stood out on the porch with him for a few minutes, and then came back in and waited at the window, watching him leave. With a perplexed look, she turned and said he had stopped by with a question about billing information.

"More like to nose around," Melinda said.

Mom said it wasn't like him, but still asked, "Does he know Billy?"

Billy was Melinda's estranged husband. Estranged, ha. More like nuts. He came at her with a pipe wrench three days ago. But I wasn't scared of him. At thirteen, I was only an inch, maybe two, shorter than him. But Melinda was scared and had been staying with us ever since. She was an old friend of the family. Mom knew her mother from way back.

She had no choice in leaving, Mom had been reassuring her every day. He was violent. What would have happened if she had stayed? Her children were safe with her mother-in-law for the time being. She would have her day in court. She already had an appointment with an attorney. Mom was running out of things to say.

As soon as she sat down, Barfy started barking again. Mom, figuring it was Skip again, went to the window with less concern in her step.

"Oh there he is!" she cried out.

I got up and ran over just in time to see Billy Johnston sneaking past our house. He had his hands jammed in his pockets and his collar turned up, hiding his stuck-out, ugly ears. As he passed, he was glancing over, trying to get a look at Melinda.

"Oh, that man," my mother said, anger shuddering through her voice. "Jason, now you stay back."

I stepped back and stood with Melinda in the middle of the living room, while Mom went on looking out. He was going on up the alley, she said. In the same breath, she asked Melinda if she thought he would be violent.

"If he's been drinking," she said.

When I started upstairs, Mom called after me, wanting to know where I was going. I was looking for my bat, I called down. I thought I had left it near her rocker, but all I found was a yardstick in the corner.

As I was coming back down, we heard glass breaking behind the house. Mom, her face lined with fear, told us to stay put. She stepped out back and stood on the steps, then came back in moments later, saying that if he was out there, she sure couldn't see him. She didn't see anything broken, either. She re-bolted the back door, and three of us stood in the kitchen, the safest part of the house, wondering what we should do next. Mom said she ought to call the police.

Just then, Barfy let out another terrific racket, Mom rushed to the window, and I followed. Billy Johnston was on our steps! He was already halfway up, and our chained dog was lunging down at him, slobbering, half-choking himself. Melinda, meanwhile, had gone to the other window, and when Billy saw her through the blinds, he went into a fit, swearing and jabbing his finger at her. That sent Barfy into his own fit, but for all his noise, he did little good. Billy was still coming up, testing how far our mouthy dog could reach.

Mom, horrified by all his foul language, told us both to get back, but Melinda, before either of us could stop her, opened the front door and stepped out. She stood on the top step with her arms crossed—while he called her every name in the book. Mom covered her mouth. Then Billy spotted me looking over her shoulder.

"Faggot!" he hissed. "Cocksucking faggot!"

Mom let out a cry. I was scared, but I was also mesmerized. Until now I had never heard him say anything other than hello.

He went on spitting foul words, Barfy went on trying to rip out his jugular, and Melinda went on standing there, arms crossed, giving him a look that said she had married a perfectly ugly man. Meanwhile, our neighbors started gawking at the commotion, and thank God, a police car turned up the hill at that moment. Billy saw it coming, backed down the steps with a few more threats, and hurried up the alley.

I darted out the back door, Mom calling out after me. I crossed the lot and came out near the Collins's house. But Billy had disappeared, gone some other way. I checked the alley, the walk in front of the church, and the church parking lot. Nothing. I ran down the steps to Saber Street, looking from side to side.

He couldn't have gone far. I headed for the sandbars, thinking he would go there to brood. I did. Along the river, trees hung low, making it dark and shadowy under the limbs. I slowed to a walk in

the deepening sand. Then, out of the corner of my eye, I saw him—
he was standing on top of the mill ruins, glaring down at me.

He hopped down and landed just feet from me. His face up close
was a shock—bony, pale, full of whiskers—and his eyes were practically falling out they were so wet. Something popped out of his pocket when he landed and hit the large rock near us. We both looked
down at the same time. It was his pipe. The curved part lay in a spot
of sunlight, making a small shadow of itself on the stone. Around it
in the sand lay several pens, one green, another blue. There was even
a short yellow pencil with a metal compass attached to it. All this had
come out of his pocket.

He cussed as he bent down to pick it all up. His pipe, he picked
up last, and when he stood up, he tapped the bowl against his
palm, emptying out the rest of the tobacco. I was taller, even with
my shoes shifted down in the soft sand.

"I know your father, boy," he said, pointing the mouth end of
the pipe at me.

He said this as if it should mean something to me, or as if I
ought to say something back. Then, the dirtiest, ugliest, trickiest
grin broke over his face.

"Here," he said, holding out his hand, "I wanna shake your
hand."

I stood close enough to see chewing tobacco in his teeth and
white and gray whiskers all over his face. He was only in his late
thirties, Mom said.

"Take it," he said, sticking his hand closer.

I looked down at his hand as the obvious trap it was. It was
filthy except for a wedding band, which was so golden it gleamed
in the light. As gold as the steeple of St. Peter's church. On the
same finger was a grungy Band-aid.

When I refused to shake his hand, he looked at me with hateful, burnt-up eyes and tried his best to insult me, calling me a home wrecker, calling my mother and father home wreckers, all of us do-gooding bastards.

"What the hell you all got against me?" he said, falling back a step. "What? I wanna know." His face lost all its hardness, and his voice whined.

I couldn't answer him. One look at him—his skinny, unshaven face, his dirty shirt, and his hair like a mop in oil—and I knew none of my reasons was enough.

"What, you all think you're better than me cause you're from town?" he said.

If I was going to say anything to him, it would be to tell him to forget about Melinda, to have some self-respect and move on.

"I'm an electricccian," he said, slurring the word. "I worked at Colhouse."

Colhouse Industries was a big toaster and microwave plant across the state line in Maryland. He held up his hands for me to see. "I'm trained," he said. "I ain't no redneck." Then I saw a half-finished bottle of beer on the log behind him, the foam filling up the top of the bottle. Nearby were a few empty bottles.

"Look," he said, taking out his wallet. It was a black, ragged lump of leather, thick with sleeves and slots. When he tried to take out a single card, the whole grimy leather mess slipped out of his hands and cracked open in the sand. He reached down but stumbled, kicking sand all over it. When he finally got the tattered card out, he held it close to his eyes.

"WV certified for electrical construction."

He sounded like a fourth-grader reading. Then he held out the card out for me, but I wouldn't take it.

"What the hell she'd tell you about me?" he said. "That I don't work?" He stood clutching the messy wallet in his fist, an accordion of family pictures dangling down. "I work." He stepped closer.

I was on autopilot, not feeling, not reacting, blank-faced, motionless, tense inside and ready to back up if I had to.

"She's my wife!"

He screamed this so hard he knocked himself off balance, and when he stepped to the side into the deepening sand, his shoes sank in, like mine. I was thirteen. He was at least thirty, looked fifty-five, but we were the same height and I probably weighed more. I could smell beer on his breath.

"Shit, you're just a boy," he said, smiling suddenly.

He turned, stopped to reach down and grab his beer, then started staggering off, his big boots mashing holes in the sand.

"Somebody should take your mother away, boy," he said over his shoulder. His plain blue mechanic's shirt was pulled out in back. "See how it feels."

Then he stopped, turned around, and came all the way back to me, beer bottle hooked over one finger, wallet crushed in his other fist, guts of pictures hanging down.

"I'm proud to be from the mountain, boy. I'm . . . proud to . . ."

He staggered off, and this time didn't stop.

I looked down. He had dropped his wallet. Stretched across the sand, like film yanked out of a camera, was an accordion of pictures in foggy plastic sleeves. I waited until he was out of sight, then hurried over. As I stooped down and picked up the stretched out mess of pictures, I felt I was saving something mutilated. With no effort, the unfolded pictures, following the creases in plastic sleeves, fell back into a stack. I glanced around to make sure he had left, then started looking at them, one by one.

There were half a dozen Sears family photos, everyone grouped together, dressed up, and smiling. I hardly recognized them, they looked so young and thin. His daughter Terri, my age, actually looked pretty in one. There was one of Billy Junior in little green coveralls and a cap. It reminded me of Mom's baby pictures on the pie safe at home. The fake blue sky made them all seem so happy.

There was even a picture of just Billy and Melinda. He had his arm around her, and his eyes weren't black and burnt up. With his shorter beard, I could see how a woman might find him handsome. There were more and more pictures of the kids. They kept unfolding and stretching out like he'd been collecting them all his life. I stood flipping through them all until I felt a smile curving higher and higher through my cheeks.

At the beginning of all these pictures was an old black-and-white photograph of a woman. She looked familiar. Her hair was balled up on top, and she looked as glamorous as a movie star. Written on back was "Arlingdale Academy for the Arts, Fort Washington, MD. 1947."

I started going through the slots in his wallet. The leather felt as grimy inside as outside. There was an Elk Hunting Lodge parking pass, an AA code of ethics card, bits of paper with names and numbers written on them, a Mobil gas card, and a business card for Angie's Florist. There was also a Harpers Ferry Public Library card. I wanted to laugh. I had one, too, and never used it. On his social security card was his full name, William Ernest Johnston, his signature, which looked fancy for a man, and his birth date, 4/9/43. He was exactly twenty years and three months older than me. There was no driver's license or money.

I stood holding the wallet, wondering what to do with it. I thought about leaving it on the sand. Then something caught my eye. It was a sheet of lined notebook paper folded over and over until it was so small it fit wedged into the tiny inner slot of the wallet. I pulled it out and unfolded it. It was a letter that read:

Dear Melinda,

Dr. Williams says I have a mouth cancer. I am going to see a specialist in Winchester the first of the month. Mom is going to drive me since the truck tires are too bad to go that far.

Do not feel sorry for me! I am writing because I WANT to make amends. I love you and always will!! I know I am not the best man for you. You said it best when you said that people on the mountain put themselves down. I finally figured out I put myself down by drinking. My counselor at AA tells me the same thing. He is encouraging me to get my GED. His name is Ed, and guess what?—he knew Marg Baker when she lived up here.

I know you do not owe me anything, but for the sake of the children, please come back home and do not divorce me now. If I loose you, I will have nothing to go on for. You always said I never showed my feelings. You were right. But I still remember the good old days when I was working full-time and pray to God that we can have those days again. I will start going to church again if you want.

Do NOT tell mom about this letter!! You know how she is. Your loving husband,

William

P.S. I have started work on the back kitchen, as you always wanted.

I didn't know if he was more ridiculous than he was pathetic. For that reason, part of me wanted to throw both wallet and letter into the river. Instead I reread it, stopped in places by his sloppy cursive. Then I folded it up, put it back in its hiding place, and glanced back through the pictures, looking for one in particular. I found it. He was much younger. If I didn't know who he was, I would say he was a normal person. What could have gone wrong? It seemed he had so much to be proud of.

I started back to town. In the parking lot, I found a brown souvenir bag pretty much unwrinkled. I put the wallet in it and folded the edges of the bag around it, the way a clerk would. When I got home, I managed to hide the bag behind my back while Mom asked me where I had gone and what had happened. I found Melinda upstairs.

"Billy dropped this," I said, handing her the bag.

His name spooked her. Her face got crossed up with ten different expressions, and as she looked inside the bag, she seemed to expect anything from a tarantula to the Hope Diamond. When she saw his wallet, she was full of questions. I answered all to her satisfaction, except one.

"What'd you two talk about?"

"Nothing."

"Nothing?"

It was obvious I was hiding something, but I kept shrugging and saying nothing until she gave up. Then she closed the bag without taking the wallet out or even touching it.

"Aren't you going to look in it?" I said.

Lines shot down her forehead. "What for?" She held the bag out for me to give to my mother to drop off at the post office. They would mail it to him. "There's nothing in it anyway." Then she laughed bitterly. "That's always been the problem."

Rusty Clackford

* * *

Top of my list of Pipertown people to sell magazine subscriptions to was Rusty Clackford. Pipertown seemed my most fertile selling ground since Dad had his crappy property here.

As I rapped on the paint-blistered door of Rusty's whitewashed shack, I could see him through the screen window, eating. I knew from looking at him he wouldn't hear a dozen pots and pans if you dropped them at his feet. So I went to the screen window nearest him and yelled in point-blank. Still no response. His veiny, ugly profile just went on staring at the TV and chewing like a skinny dying cow. So I went around the house to the far window behind the TV, where he'd have no choice but to see me if I waved long enough.

By the time I got there, he had stood and was now teetering over to the window I had just been at. Unwisely, I started yelling out from this side of the house, too. The TV was louder over here—no chance he'd hear me. I hurried back around the house. But by the time I got back to the first window—you guessed it— the old fool was shuffling over to the second window, where I had unwisely yelled from. And no amount of additional yelling would stop him. Yelling only created sounds Rusty could never catch up to. I decided to wait it out on the front step. Eventually he'd think to check there.

Sure enough, a good five minutes later he came to the door in a dingy tee-shirt and rumpled tan pants held up with red suspenders. No socks or shoes, though.

"You here to fix my furnace?" he asked.

When he unlatched the door, I had the feeling he was mistaking me for one of my older brothers and my sales brochure under my arm for a toolbox.

Soon I was standing in his living room, looking at his orange vinyl chairs and Formica table, wondering how old they were. This house was vintage Pipertown: St. Joseph wall thermometers, washed-out cowboy prints, booger-green TV chair. On the kitchen counter was a row of Franco-American Spaghetti cans, along with cheap bowls from the Dollar General Store down in town. They looked like something for children, being big and blue, having been used a thousand times, with scratch marks all around the inside of them. The forks nearby were as light as the aluminum one in my brother's camping kit. There was also a scrunched-up half loaf of Wonder Bread—everything plain and simple. Dad wouldn't mind eating this way. Mom and Grandma would politely pass, though.

Fantasy Island was on TV, the volume up loud.

"That's my favorite show," he said. "You like it?"

I nodded, trying to be polite.

"You do? *Really?* Jen hates it."

Jen was Rusty's dead wife. All of Pipertown knew that he had been talking to her ever since she died back in 1957—the same night they discovered a second UFO in Roswell, New Mexico, whatever the connection was.

For my benefit, Rusty ambled over to the TV and turned it up even more.

"That man there, he misses his child," he started explaining. "He plays that old fart on *The Waltons*." He turned to me. "You like that too?"

I found myself nodding and speaking up, practically yelling— "Dad likes *The Waltons* because it takes place near here!"

Actually, it took place about two hours away by car, over in Virginia. But close enough for Dad. Mountain, he always said, was mountain.

"What?" Rusty called back, face strained, hand cocked to his ear.

I couldn't yell the whole sentence at him again. This was a horrible way to talk. So I just looked back at the TV.

A moment later, Rusty left the room and came teetering back with a TV tray for me, to my surprise, which I helped him set up. When he brought me a fork, he was wobbling so badly I expected him to fall and stab himself with it. It was then I noticed all the cigarette burns in the carpet. Looked like a pail of fishing worms had been cooked into the floor.

Eventually we sat down to eat. Rusty was the oldest-looking man I ever saw. Even the sweat on his forehead looked a hundred years old. His fingertips were yellowed from cigarettes—blackened, too, Dad said from matches he'd light and forget he had lit.

"So?" he said, trying to wrap a few strands of spaghetti around his fork, "people always making a big thing out of mountain life."

I had no idea where this remark came from, but I nodded anyway. For a moment, I almost wished my father could see me sitting here with Rusty. He always said having dinner with any family in Pipertown on any night of the week was the best mark of a man, even if the spaghetti was stone-cold inside. The one time Dad's car stalled on a mountain road near here, half the families from every hollow around came out to help. They wallowed under his car, rooting around for the problem, practically pushing the old clunker up onto a jack themselves. With the world gone crazy everywhere else, Dad felt an admiration for them on the highest level.

"You like living up here?" Rusty asked.

I thought, briefly, of trying to point out that, technically, we didn't live up here yet, but decided just to nod instead.

"You do?" he asked back.

"They're a bunch of snooty Methodists down in town!" I shouted at him.

"What?"

I had to look back at the TV and simply not answer him. Otherwise, I'd be shouting at him for the next half hour, just for one sentence. Besides, I was glad he didn't hear me betray my mother with that remark. At the commercial, I looked over at him again.

"You know Annie?" I asked right in his ear.

He looked at me, smiled, and nodded.

"She's nice, isn't she?" I said.

He went on smiling and nodding. Old fool. He had no idea what I was saying. Annie was a girl who lived down in town.

"You know Flabby Abby?" I asked next.

Again he smiled and nodded.

"Skeet the Cheat?"

Another nod. Another stupid smile.

"Carlin the Marlin?"

Nod. Smile.

"Bell from Hell?"

I was naming Pipertown's roughest characters. They sat in the rocks down at the community water pipe, knees pulled up to their chins, cigarettes smoldering from their fingertips, long hair, goatees, tattoos—a bunch of gargoyles in dirty jeans.

I went on for minutes, from "Annie Fanny" to "Mrs. Hickle

Pickle." It was actually cool, talking to someone who couldn't hear you. You could say whatever you wanted—cuss words, even lies.

"Abby's pretty, isn't she?"

Nod. Smile.

"Would you boink her?"

Nod. Smile. Old fool.

Then I looked at him for a long moment. All the while, I could feel my sales brochure on the floor leaning against my leg.

"Dad says I'd be better off as a girl."

I listened to my voice escape into his house. Rusty nodded the same fool nod.

"Says being an artist is sissy stuff," I went on.

He looked at me with his watery, red eyes.

"Says he wishes I'd never been born."

When he went on making a fuss with his fork in the crappy spaghetti, I let it fly.

"Fuck Harpers Ferry! *Fuck, fuck, fuck.* Shit town full of losers."

I sat looking at the side of his head. Deaf fool.

"You know Deedee? *Deedee peepee. Deedee creepy. Deedee weepy.*"

I heard my horrible words disappear into silence. Who was the fool now?

Meanwhile, on TV, Ricardo Montalban was walking along a beach with the actor who played Grandpa Walton, who was telling him about his dead child.

"Jenny," he said, "was my only reason for living."

Ricardo Montalban stopped, turned to him, and said in a grand way. "Then, my dear Mr. Collins, you have that reason yet again."

Suddenly, walking up from the surf behind Mr. Collins appeared his young daughter, alive again. The old man turned, showed great surprise, embraced the child, and broke into tears.

Music rolled up like the surf. When Mr. Collins turned back to thank Ricardo Montalban, he was gone.

"Oh, ain't that nice," Rusty said, showing all his bad teeth, Franco-American style. He sat looking at me for a moment. "Bet you wish your fantasy would come true like that, huh?"

Fork stopped in mid-stair, I looked at him.

"What?"

"Why, that girl Abby?" he said, as clear as a bell, slowly standing to leave the table.

I went frozen. Shit and double shit. Dad said sometimes Rusty could actually hear. I looked back at the TV, clammed up for good. How much had he heard? All of it, I was afraid.

Next on TV Land was *Marcus Welby, M.D.* I was thinking of how to leave politely when moments later Rusty appeared in hallway, holding a white-splattered paint can by its wire handle.

"You can paint, can't you, son?"

I sat looking at him from behind my TV tray, dirty plate in front of me, belly full of Franco-American spaghetti and buttered bread, *Marcus Welby, M.D.* now on the TV. Never mind the glossy *DMA Magazine Subscription Clearinghouse* packet on my lap, but, yes, I could paint with Sherwin-Williams.

Just like that, I found myself following him up narrow steps, into sunlight blasting through a little window covered in a white sheer matted with flies and moths. It took some pulling and yanking, but I got the little paint-flaked sash up without breaking the old panes, although big chunks of caulking rained down everywhere.

"Jen!" Rusty called down the steps. "Bring up the dust pan!" Then he turned to me, his wrinkled old face glistening from the climb. "I started scraping out there last summer, but, lord, I couldn't finish." Then he turned and called down the steps again. "And a broom, hon!"

Out the little window I climbed, stepping onto a faded silver tin roof that made popping and buckling sounds under my sneakers. I saw all the rocks my brother Greg had chucked up here, and kicked them off. Rusty, arm trembling, handed me the paint can through the window, which I then shook up in front of him like a hardware store paint-shaker, to show off my strength. Then, using a screwdriver left on the sill for so long the rain had washed a rust trail from it down the side of the house, I expertly pried off the lid. Rich silver paint appeared, swimming in tiny bubbles. Next, Rusty handed me a paint brush, the cheap kind with a cream-colored plastic handle and shiny black synthetic bristles—a damn Wal-Mart brush, my father would gripe. Trying to look like an expert, I bent the bristles across my palm a few times, like an artist warming up, then dipped them in. Out of the corner of my eye I saw Rusty watching as I brushed my strokes to perfection, drawing the sparking paint down, then back, spreading it as far as it would go, careful not to let it build up high on the bristles, as Dad always told us.

"Bring up some iced tea, Jen!" he yelled down, this time from outside the house.

As I went on painting, pulling the sparking silver paint down and back, spreading it over rust and old paint alike, the happiness I suddenly felt spread over me with every stroke. Painting a roof in Pipertown? It was strangely therapeutic. I found myself glancing out over the little houses in the distance. If only my father knew what I was doing now, he'd be proud of me for once. He'd approve of me for once. Here I was, putting myself to good use, for good people.

I turned and looked down at the window below.

"And a rag, too, Mrs. Clackford!" I shouted down.

Rusty looked at me, smiled, and nodded, and I went on painting.

Mountain Wake

***

Junior's wake was held at his sister's house, a little stick-and-plywood structure back off the main road, with a porch that was nothing more than painted two-by-fours holding up a sheet of corrugated tin. Dad drove us in. Even though he was still living on the mountain, Mom said we should be together as a family when we go honor the dead. Surrounding the shack were junk cars overgrown with a weird, bright-green ivy that, in spotting hoods and trunks, made them look like the backs of tortoises. Dad's car, free of such foliage, finally looked like a new car by comparison.

Our father led the way inside, with Mom in the rear, down a narrow hall made all the narrower by thick old wicker picture frames hanging from long wires and leaning out from the wall. In a small back room crowded with heavy-looking dressers, Junior lay dead on a bed.

"Oh, good heavens," Mom said, starting to turn around, hand over her mouth, as if blocking a foul smell, which didn't actually exist.

Junior didn't look peaceful and sleeping. He looked wretched and dead. But he had looked wretched and dead most of his life, and he just looked more so now. He was stretched out on a fluffy baby-blue blanket, which looked to me like an electric blanket, and was wearing a red-striped polyester shirt and green bowling pants. My older brother Andy, showing no fear of the cadaver, stood over him, as if eager to throw him around like an old scarecrow. Dad let out a complaint right away, wanting to know who in the hell dressed him in those colors.

"And another thing—who in the hell put a quarter over one eye and a dime on the other?" he said, turning to the hall where the old woman who was Junior's sister had last been standing.

"I did, Bill," said a familiar voice.

Johnny Kell, giving our mother a start, appeared in the doorway, his dirty blonde hair all the longer and his face unshaven and gritty. The best he could dress up for the occasion was to wear a heavy purple sweater with his holey jeans, this in the middle of May.

"Damn it, Johnny," said our father, "you couldn't find two dimes or two quarters? Or even two pennies?"

"Hell, Bill, he don't know the difference," Johnny said, pointing at the corpse. "Besides, he owes me."

Dad stood looking at him.

"Owes you?"

"Yeah, ten bucks for a carton of coffin nails. So I'm being generous, I figure."

Dad looked at him utterly blank-faced for a long moment. Then, out it came—our father's super-stretched, famous Pipertown laugh, gold in the corner of his mouth looking like earrings, a laugh I hadn't seen since I was little. Andy and Greg burst into snickers. The most I would do was grin. Mom stood shaking her head at the inappropriateness of it all.

Kell snapped the tab on a beer can—*psst!*, and took a gurgle of it right in front of us and the honored dead, in such a way we could see the clear watery beer gurgling into his mouth like spring water over rocks. When he let out a long burp, Andy snotted all over himself. This was by no means a proper wake at St. Peter's in town.

Kell stood smiling, his teeth as odd and discolored as stones in a kaleidoscope.

"Hey, bud," he said, stepping up and slapping our father on the back, "you a fine mailman." The crazy longhair went on grinning, showing a green front tooth, yellow lower teeth, and something black and silver on the side. "Through rain, snow, and shit, here comes Bill with our bills!"

Over the next half hour, while Dad helped Junior's sister fix her toilet, my brothers and I stood outside on the front porch, the boards of which felt as flimsy as a rotten raft. Half of Pipertown came through the trees, all on foot. One guy brought a Wal-Mart bag full of Macintosh apples. Another a pipe wrench he had borrowed from Junior seventeen years ago. They looked us over, then filed on inside, soon returning with a Schaeffer beer each, which Kell was handing out by the body like free caps at a baseball game. The porch was filled with men drinking beer when Dad came out with a toilet plunger to shake off. At this point, Mom, understandably, preferred to sit in the car.

"Them your boys there, Bill?" asked an old man in a funny brown suit with big white stitches running up the sleeves and collar.

"Yeah, Harvey, that's Andy there, the tallest," said Dad. "Greg in the middle. And Jason. He takes after his mother."

"Fine-looking boys."

The old men around the porch made a few nods. Our father was nobody to say otherwise to. After all, he brought them their disability checks, so they better be nice to him or he might misplace their mail. More than that, he was from across the river, from Harpers Ferry where all the fancy city folk went, so he was no hick to laugh at. That, and the fact he kept a gun under his seat.

"Andy here," Dad said, "can run the mile in under—what, Andy—five minutes?"

For a moment, my brother looked as if he had forgotten to speak.

"Four fifty-two," he said.

"Just four fifty-two?" Dad asked back. "You sure? I thought it was four twenty-something."

Andy stood frozen.

"And Greg here," Dad went on, "won some damn school spelling bee on the word—what the hell was it?"

"Autochthonous," Greg said, with just a second delay.

Dad stood smiling.

"Spell it."

Greg went into action, rattling off the 13 lucky letters that had earned him a blue ribbon, back in junior high: "A-u-t-o-c-h-t-h-o-n-o-u-s."

The whiskered old men stood gawking as if they couldn't spell dummy or dipstick.

"And Jason—hell, he won the county fair art contest three years ago."

"Two," I said.

"Two, okay."

By now, the only sound on the porch was that of one of the old-timers sucking his tobacco pipe dry. That, and amazement rattling around in my brothers' and my hearts like a steel ball in an empty spray-paint can. Junior was dead, and our father was proud of us. Mom was sitting in the car.

John Brown the Quaker

* * *

One evening, down in Harpers Ferry, my new neighbors the Collinses and I piled into their Fiat and headed up High Street. Luke and Alex, who were my age, started passing a small can of makeup back and forth, painting their faces brown. We were off to play slave children in a dress rehearsal of a play about John Brown. I slid down in the seat, in case Dad drove by. Luke handed me the makeup, which looked like shoe polish, and started laughing as I smeared it down my cheeks. I had lumps of it on my lips and gobs hanging from my eyelashes. By the time we turned up Philmore Street, the three of us were brown-faced with white ears. Walter, the oldest, didn't put any on. He sat talking to his father like a grown-up.

Philmore Street was full of nice old houses. My family didn't know anyone up here because these people, like the Collinses, worked for the park service and drove new cars. This was historic Harpers Ferry, and my family lived down the hill, with a hundred tacky souvenir shops jammed around us. All day long was the buzz of tourists in every nook and cranny on the street. Over the years, it had a way of crushing us down, making us unfriendly. We were ashamed of our drab little house beside the big restored park buildings, and we were hostile toward tourists. When my brother shot a hole in the wax museum window across the street with a pellet gun and nicked the figure of John Brown across the pants leg, Dad asked how come he didn't aim for the head.

But when the Collinses moved in next door a few months back, that all changed. Mr. Collins was the first man in years to go out of his way to be neighborly to my father. He came over to Dad's work-shop and asked him for advice on home repairs. Dad was all busi-ness at first, telling the younger man what he had to do to replace this or that, step-by-step until the end. Mr. Collins always had the look of not listening at all, but of trying to figure Dad out, as if he were some kind of puzzle to him.

Dad took to him, and soon they started doing everything togeth-er. Mr. Collins had an old WWI motorcycle with a sidecar that the two tinkered on in the evenings. You should have seen our father stuffed down in this sidecar, an old German motorcycle helmet over his head, the two of them riding past the house, tourists look-ing on. He was having the time of his life.

So was I, more than my brothers. It wasn't that I felt worthier than them to be reading Shakespeare with Mr. Collins. I was just better than they were at laughing when Mr. Collins did, better at looking serious at the right times, too. When I watched Alex and Luke read together from a playbook, I didn't laugh or think they were sissies—I knew they were kinder to each other, closer, than my brothers and I would ever be. Being in a play about John Brown was just another example of how different this family was from any I had ever known.

We pulled up to a stone house not much bigger than ours, with fancy electric candles in every window, making it look like Christ-mas. Even in the evening light, the mortar was as white as the backs of my sneakers, and the columns glistened with green paint.

This was what Mom wanted to do with our house—make it look like something in a tourism brochure.

A fat man with a pink face opened the door and was all smiles for Mr. Collins and even gave him a hug. I recognized him as a big author around town. He wrote ghost stories about Harpers Ferry and Antietam. Dad said he was full of nonsense. Mom said he took care of his mother well.

"I see you all came ready," he said, looking at the three of us.

We went inside to a room full of people dressed up like on Halloween. There was a man in a farmer's overalls, with the same brown makeup on his face, only darker. He had done something to his hair, too, to make it like an Afro. Still I recognized him. He worked in the visitor's center. My brothers and I bent the antenna off his jeep. With him was the lady who worked in the park bookstore. She was wearing an old-time dress. Mom and I saw her around town, talking only to important people. Mom said she certainly was aloof, which meant snotty. There were others I knew: the man who lived right behind us and the architect for the park Dad didn't like because he double-parked his Mercedes everywhere. Lee Jackson, who owned nearly every souvenir shop on the hill, was here, too. He had on an old flop hat. I couldn't imagine what part he was playing. There was Dave Spiner, another park employee who had moved in just up the street, in a house Mom said had once belonged to a real Harpers Ferry family, the Jenkins, before they were forced out. Dad called him a do-gooder, so my brothers poured kerosene on his marigolds.

Around the room were all these people who were my neighbors but who my family never spoke to and my brothers and I had harmed in some way. Fear was the size of a pumpkin in my chest.

But as I looked around at everyone talking and laughing, I began to realize that no one recognized me under my brown makeup.

I was standing right beside Lee Jackson, the most important man in town, and didn't have to feel bad. It was like on Halloween when, wearing my Casper the Friendly Ghost mask, I could knock on any door in town and not feel ashamed.

The house was small like ours, with a low ceiling and cramped stairs in the corner, but much nicer, with bright lights, dark furniture, and fancy rugs. Mom tried to say that the reason Dad forbid us from having friends over to our house was that it was too small, but here was a house the same size, and half of Harpers Ferry was standing in it. There was the gray-haired lady who ran the herb shop on Potomac Street. There was a man in a Civil War uniform. Alex ran up to him and started touching his sword. Walter was already talking to a girl in a polka-dotted dress.

Some time later, Mr. Collins appeared from a side room wearing an old nightgown, a phony beard, and a gray bandana spotted with fake blood. He looked like a pirate, not John Brown. When he lay down on the sofa, everyone else took their places, too. The room became quiet. Some had playbooks out. Then a tall man wearing what looked like Dracula's cape came in and sat in a fancy chair in the middle of the room. He looked more like John Brown. Near him was a man holding a nightstick. I recognized him as the park ranger who lived in Dotty Riley's old place. According to Walter, he had played for the Chicago White Sox when he was younger. The Civil War soldier was behind him, standing like a guard. Everyone else was sitting in folding chairs. Alex, Luke, and I went up to the sofa, where we knelt in a row as if on the kneeler in church. Alex knew our cue, and we didn't have speaking parts, so I wasn't worried.

Then the man in Dracula's cape started speaking, reading a list of charges against John Brown, which included everything from destruction of property to treason. The fat man with the pink face then spoke at length, too, in a funny, overdone voice, pointing a Bible at Mr. Collins and saying to the people in the folding chairs that he ought to be judged by the law of God and the land. It went on this way for some time, with everyone getting a chance to point their finger at Mr. Collins and use words like guilty and everlasting punishment.

Then Mr. Collins sat up and, with his arm outstretched, started speaking to the ceiling in a wavering voice. He spoke in long sentences that rose and fell like mountains and valleys. He said he had no consciousness of guilt and that he regretted the weakness of man. He mentioned places like Missouri and Canada and spoke of trying to free slaves without violence.

". . . I have yet another objection," he said, "and that is, it is unjust I should suffer such a penalty . . . had I so interfered in behalf of the rich, the powerful, the intelligent, the so called great, either father, mother, brother, sister, wife, or children—" He paused as one by one, Alex, Luke, and I stepped forward on our knees and placed our hands on his. "—it would have been all right, and every man in this court would have deemed it an act worthy of reward rather than punishment."

In reverse order, we stepped back, and Mr. Collins went on speaking, saying he was following God's commandment. When he finished, Lee Jackson in his flop hat stood and spoke, saying the accused was innocent in the eyes of God. Luke whispered that he was playing Oliver Brown, one of John Brown's sons. The man in the black cape then rambled on for some time about crimes against humanity and their consequences. He spoke for so long that Alex sat cross-legged on the floor. So Luke and I did, too. When he finished by saying Mr. Collins should be hanged by the neck until dead, Walter stood up and cheered loudly. That was his only part in the play, an angry spectator.

Then everyone started clapping, smiling, and looking around at one another. Mr. Collins, the fatally wounded John Brown, stood, pulled off his phony beard, and bowed. The fat man, raising his wine glass, said he thought it was one of their best rehearsals yet. Soon someone commented that the slave children deserved a hand, too. Niles's sons were all fine budding actors, he said. All eyes were on us, and everyone clapped again. Then, I could feel it coming. A lady behind me remarked that I wasn't one of Niles's sons.

"Who's that boy?" she whispered.

Others started asking, too. Mr. Collins told them my name, and I could hear the murmurs. Bill Stevens's son? What's he doing here? I saw Lee Jackson staring hard at me. When he came to our door about buying our house, Dad said something that gave him a red face.

"Bill Stevens," Lee Jackson said loud and clear, "now he'd make a perfect John Brown!"

Everyone laughed, including Luke. The sound was like a thousand crushed cans in my ears. I could feel the makeup baking on my face. It was true. My father was always angry and yelling like John Brown, but the funny thing was, he didn't like blacks.

"Or at least a perfect conspirator," added the fat man, thinking he was funny.

The man dressed up as the Civil War soldier said he had heard that Bill Stevens had a gun collection that would rival Grant's 42nd militia. Everyone laughed again. I looked at Mr. Collins, but he looked almost as embarrassed and helpless as I was. All I could do was laugh along, the makeup on my face cracking in a thousand places—across the forehead, around the chin.

"Is that the little house across from the wax museum?" asked the girl beside Walter. "The one with that noisy black dog in front? Someone lives there?"

"Yes, can you believe it, someone lives there," Lee Jackson said, enjoying himself.

I hated him. I wished I had hung a thousand shrunken heads around his porch, not just one.

Then everyone started speaking as if I weren't there, asking one another how long our house had been in the family, why we had not sold it when everyone around us had, and what it must be like to be the only native family left so far down the hill. The fat man, whose house this was, said our house actually predated his and most in the lower part of town because it was built as part of the original ferry operation. The aloof woman added that she knew for a fact our house had been used as a hospital during the Civil War. She also thought it had been part of the church at the turn of the century. The gray-haired lady who ran the herb shop, though she was no fan of Lee Jackson, did not hesitate to bring up the fact that our house was the only one on the street that did not decorate for Old Tyme Christmas. When she asked my father to participate, to put just a few strands of garland around the porch columns, he was not afraid to be rude, she said.

"Well, they're good neighbors now," Mr. Collins tried to tell them.

I did not need ears to hear the grumbling. In my mind, the charges against my father were as lengthy as those against John Brown—unneighborliness, treason against the National Park Service, inciting rebellion in his children and the destruction of park property, and general insurrection. And just as everyone had found John Brown guilty, so they would find my father guilty. Guilty! Guilty! I could see it on their faces. *He* invited no one into his house and went to see no one at theirs, either. *He* didn't wave, blow his horn, or nod. All he gave his neighbors was a shut door and drawn blinds. And the mischief—broken windows, vandalized mailboxes, trash in the yards. Everyone knew who was responsible for that.

In one great burst, I spoke up. "He always wanted to be a sea captain!"

For the longest time, whenever my father said this, I believed him. I would imagine him on a ship, turning the big wheel, the waves splashing over him. I was excited to think of him no longer riding around in our old car all day, delivering mail and collecting rubber bands on the gearshift. But whenever I got excited for him, he would just shake his head at me, as if I were the dumbest kid in the world. Mom said he was being sarcastic. He should have *never wanted* to be a sea captain, was what he meant. When I asked why, he said that just because a person wanted something didn't mean he had the right to want it. He said this as if trying to teach me one of the Ten Commandments.

The gray-haired lady, sitting in a red metal chair, looked about to laugh. "A sea captain? Working for the post office?"

"John Brown worked as a postmaster at one time," said Mr. Collins.

"John Brown had a noble cause, Niles."

"And I was just a cook in the army," he said back. "Just a lowly cook, Ida."

Trying to make light of it all, he asked me what kind of boat my father wanted to captain. A fishing vessel? A navy ship? But I couldn't remember, and the gray-haired lady was not so easily turned aside by his good mood. A man who makes himself so unfriendly, she said, should move for everyone's sake, his children's especially.

Alex spoke up, playing into her disdain.

"His father won't allow them in any of the shops, either."

Alex wasn't trying to be mean. He liked to speak up, and I could tell he was defending me.

Not allowed in any shops? How could a father be so strict? It must be just awful for me, someone said.

"Well don't blame this boy," said the man playing the judge.

"Here, here!" said Walter, standing up and playing the angry spectator once again.

The man playing one of John Brown's sons asked with a laugh why he himself didn't get the same leniency. I recognized him finally. I had egged his jeep once.

Around the room, they had other questions for me—how long had my father been working for the post office? Where was he raised? I wasn't surprised they knew so little about him. Dad was like one of those black iron statues down on Shenandoah Street no one could step close to because of the thorny bushes around them. Mr. Collins spoke up for me, telling them that my father had grown up in the big white house on River Road and that he had been more or less raised by the Brothers at the adjacent church school, which the fat man with the wine glass knew for a fact had been run by Jesuits. Together, they might as well have said John Brown was a Quaker.

The gray-haired lady reared back and said, "Bill Stevens raised by Jesuits?"

They had questions about my mother, too. Everyone knew her mother, Margaret Jennings, town recorder for many years. This led to a big question—how in the world had my parents met? My brothers and I could never imagine it, either, but we had photos albums at home to prove it. There was our father, slim, young-faced, holding us as babies. It was a sight that creased us down the middle.

Then, from one of the park people came the worst question of all.

"Are you all really related to Ricky Hardaway?"

Ricky Hardaway was a kind of Oliver Twist in our family, only worse, with no happy ending. He was related to us somehow, on Dad's side of the family, but no one wanted to know how exactly. His last name wasn't Stevens, which was helpful in hiding that he was related to us. As many times as he went to jail, he kept coming back, popping up in town with the worst characters, in the most run-down cars. He had broken into every shop at least once, so if a ranger jeep wasn't following him around, a cop car was.

I felt the pressure in my face and said the only thing I could think of: "Dad said we're related to John Wilkes Booth."

The room burst out—cheers and boos from every direction. There were stunned faces, horrified ones, smiles, the whole Halloween collection. Mostly they laughed and pointed at Mr. Collins, whose face had gone red with a shine.

"Look out, Niles! You brought a young assassin in our midst," said the fat man with the wine glass. History is doomed to repeat itself, he went on in a loud, silly voice.

"Oh, how uncanny," exclaimed the gray-haired lady, shaking her head.

Fitting, ironic, said others. Luke was looking at me as if I had just made a fool of myself. He tried to whisper something in my ear, but I couldn't hear. When all the hoopla settled down, I learned that John Wilkes Booth had not only witnessed John Brown's hanging, but he had quit acting to join a Richmond militia for the sole purpose of being present at the event. Mr. Collins was looking at me as if this were 1859, and I had hanged myself.

"Jason," he said, "are you all really related to John Wilkes Booth?"

My mom said he was something like a fourteenth cousin five times removed. Grandma Stevens had him as far back as a twenty-second cousin twelve times removed. Either way, he was back there somewhere in time. Dad and Uncle Dave talked about how it made us famous. It was one of the rare times anyone in my family laughed. It was a hit in my history class, too. When you're learning about one president, one explorer, and one inventor after another, you forget who shot Abe Lincoln and who invented the cotton gin. Your ear gets lazy with famous names. Tracy Owens met Scott Baio at the Silver City Mall, and I was related to John Wilkes Booth. It all seemed even-steven to me.

But as far as this room was concerned, I might as well have said I killed Kennedy.

"Well if you all are related to John Wilkes Booth," said the gray-haired lady, "then I shouldn't be surprised you're related to Ricky Hardaway."

Lee Jackson was quick to agree. Lincoln was a good guy toward blacks, so it was no surprise that my racist father's kin had done him in. At least the fat man said I had acting in my blood.

Mr. Collins put up his hands again.

"I have news for you all," he said. "*I* have a notorious relative in my family, too."

The room quieted down. They could see he was serious. Mr. Collins looked at Luke and Alex, who both nodded. So did Andy, out in the audience.

"Well, who?" someone shouted.

"Leon Czolgosz."

"Who?" laughed the blacksmith.

President William McKinley's assassin, someone answered. Mr. Collins was straight-faced when he said his great-great-great-great grandmother was a Polish-Russian immigrant named Eva Czolgosz—Leon Czolgosz's niece.

Suddenly, around the room everyone told which notorious person they were related to. We had cousins of Jesse James, Al Capone, and even King George IV. We had relatives of Lizzie Borden, Princess Caroline, and someone named Axis Sally. All in all, two presidential assassins, an outlaw, a murderess, a traitor, along with half a dozen tyrants and gangsters. My, we certainly had the infamous well-represented in Harpers Ferry, someone commented.

"Well, John Brown," said the gray-haired lady, "I don't know what to think of any of my neighbors now."

She was just jealous because she wasn't related to anybody bad. I was just happy I had more than Ricky Hardaway's vandalism in my blood.

Mr. Collins raised his hands again and looked around the room slowly. *We* are all outsiders to somebody, he said. He spoke in hills and valleys, as if still in his part. He said my father's name as if he could see him from many angles, as if Dad stood in the middle of a circle of mirrors.

"If it is deemed necessary," he started saying in his John Brown voice, "that I should forfeit my life for the furtherance of the ends of justice . . ." He looked up as if speaking to God. ". . . and mingle my blood further with the blood of my children . . ."

"Oh, Niles," said the gray-haired lady, chuckling.

". . . and with the blood of millions in this slave country whose rights—" Mr. Collins himself couldn't hold back a grin. "—are disregarded by wicked, cruel, and unjust enactments. I submit—so let it be done!"

Carter

***

It was summer vacation, and my brother Andy and I spent most days at our Uncle Greg's lake cabin. I got to ride the mini-bike our uncle had given us. It was gold-colored and started like a lawn mower, by pulling a rope. It sounded like a chain saw and smoked like one, too. I zipped around by myself, up and down the roads through the woods, flat-out, leaving blue smoke in the trees.

One day, I took the road through the pine groves above the spring and followed it around to the south end of Lakeside Estates. It was late in the afternoon and the road was in shade. I was building up speed as I came out of a turn when I found myself heading straight into a deer frozen in the road. I froze, too, and went off the road and into greenbriers. The deer bolted away, I spilled off the bike, and the greenbriers ripped through my jeans. The bike cut off and wouldn't restart.

As I sat rubbing my leg, the woods became quiet around me. I looked up and imagined Lisa coming toward me through the trees. Lisa was the girl I loved. She had lived over this way for a long while, until two months ago, when she and her parents moved to Omaha for her father's job. The grown-up trees and brush at the south end now seemed an impenetrable barrier, a fortress of thick and spindly trunks alike. Bark looked bitter brown. Roots were grimy and sinister. The canopy over the land was a sickening array of blotches. She would appear behind no tree. She would wave to me from no clearing. She was gone.

When I started walking the mini-bike, I realized I was not exactly where I thought I was. I looked up, and rising up in front of me like another lost monument in these woods was a great A-frame house.

I had never been this close to one before. The roof ran down to the ground like a teepee, but basically it was a great triangle, with the parts of a normal house—roof, porch, windows—fit onto it, like pieces of a toy.

Cool. Weird. I had always loved the idea of a house shaped like an "A," the A being the superior grade, the first letter, and a house boldly taking its shape from it. I stepped closer to it, watching it rise higher and higher above me. This was another kind of fairy tale, a fairy tale with flair. God, if he did exist, lived in this house— he had style, plopping a steeple on the ground this way, giving it tinted windows, then staining the pine.

There was no car in the driveway that led up to it from the right. I found its chimney, a pipe that stood where a cross would stand on a church. No smoke was coming from it.

As I stepped onto a large deck built right into the forest, I saw myself in the tinted glass—it looked back at me with an unblinking eye, as if the whole house were something alien and alive. For me, houses were alive. They watched me. All houses did.

I stepped lightly across the deck, looking down at the boards and wondering briefly what my father would think of the con-struction. I was impressed that they did not creak. He was always commenting on things like that. I looked up and around at the shingles on the roof and large overhang in front of me and thought how strange it was to walk at roof level. I stopped and put my hand against the coarse wood shingles, imagining that I could tell whether someone was home, as if putting my ear to a rail to hear a train coming. I walked up to the glass and pressed my face against it and strained to see in, but the inside was too dim, and I could make out only the faint outlines of furniture. I sat on a lounge chair and looked down at the leaves and pine needles on the deck. I sat here for what seemed the longest time, pretending I lived here. I wished I had a broom. I would have swept off the deck for whoever did live here. I was always wishing weird things like that.

I stood and started turning doorknobs and pulling against the glass sliding doors. My grandmother's ranch house had a sliding glass door, so I knew how it worked. Then, just as I sat down again, I heard the door closest to me slide open. I turned to catch a glimpse of an old man in yellow pants appearing from behind the glass. He said hello in a voice that did not sound as if he wanted to chase me away, and I might have stopped running if I weren't already bolting across the deck. Instead, I dashed into the woods and glanced back from a distance. He was old and fat, wearing ridiculous yellow pants. I recognized him. Carter Randolph! The old fag from town. He watched me jog out of sight.

I wandered around in the woods for a while, hearing his voice in my head.

I crept back the very next evening and watched the A-frame from the trees. I saw a car in the driveway this time—the yellow car that had been beside Lisa's house so many times, big and bright yellow like his pants, and new looking. I wondered where it had been the evening before.

Crouched in the trees, I made out barely a glint of light in the grid of tinted glass that made up the rear of the house. I thought that this light looked like a candle burning in a prison cell.

I surprised myself by standing out in the open where anyone behind the black glass could see me. For a while, nothing happened. Then he surprised me by being on the lane to the right. He was walking a dog. "Hello," he called out.

He was not so close as he had been yesterday, but even from a distance I could see a look of amusement on his face. He wore the same lemon-colored pants, too.

"Are you Squanto?" I heard him ask.

I knew who Squanto was and didn't think he was very funny. He knew who I really was. I said I was looking for the Kennedy place. He nodded in the right direction, so I hurried back into the trees.

I sneaked back later that same evening. In the dusk, I could clearly see lights on in his house, and as I crept closer, I heard music, too. It sounded like Beethoven or something fancy like that. It was playing louder than the house was thick, it seemed, as if bursting through the seams in the wood.

With darkness behind me, I had full advantage and crept close, in bold, outright steps. I saw him inside. He was sprawled out on the sofa, reading a thick book. He wore glasses and had on the same lemon-colored pants from earlier. What kind of man wore lemon-colored pants?

I crouched by the glass and looked around the room. It was a fine room, as modern ones went, having a fluffy TV chair, a glass coffee table, and plenty of abstract pictures in thin frames on the walls. The rear wall looked made of rounded timbers, like a log cabin, but there were only rafters where a ceiling should be.

I watched him read for a long while. Every now and then, he looked off as if he were thinking. Then, at all once, he sat up and looked right at me, or at least he seemed to. He had that thinking expression on as he stared in my direction. He picked up a pack of cigarettes off the coffee table, lit one, and blew smoke high into the air before lying back down and continuing reading. Funny how he lay on the sofa like someone in a bathtub. Funny, too, how he lay there in a house with no blinds, as if he wanted me to see in. Sometime later, when I was settled in a sitting position by the glass, I felt a twitching against my leg and looked down. His dog! It was looking up at me with its dopey brown eyes. I pushed it away, but it just stood there and stared at me, as if wondering what I was doing. I figured I better leave, and I left quickly, so it wouldn't follow me. It was embarrassing to be caught by a dumb dog.

The next evening I walked right in front of his house in broad daylight, as if I lived on the lane, too. I had to walk back and forth a dozen times before he came outside, his dog on a leash. He had the look of making a formal appearance to greet me. "Find it yet?" he called out.

I stopped and looked at him.

"The rabbit, Alice?" he said.

He walked across the yard toward me and looked down at his dog as it wandered up to me and started sniffing my shoes.

"Wonder what he smells?" he said, as if asking himself this question. Then he looked at me with his goofy old face.

I couldn't tell if he was asking me a question or not.

He asked me how my mother was, whom he knew from the library in town, I guess, and I just shrugged. He told me his dog's name, but I didn't hear it. He told me something else, too, that I didn't hear. All I heard was a buzzing in my head.

I stood staring down at his legs. He was wearing those long, tan shorts that a big-game African hunter wears, but he had the ugliest shins I had ever seen. Pale, blotchy shins. He also had small calf muscles, too, so slender and weak looking that I wondered how he was able to walk. He said something else, and I heard enough of it to know that he saw me looking at his legs and that he, too, thought they were funny looking.

"Is that a poodle?" I asked.

"Cocker Spaniel."

When I said nothing else, he looked around at the trees from where I had come and said he liked his mountain neighbors. He named one. Mr. Powell.

"Lovely man, Hank," he said.

I probably only stared, but it felt as if I gawked. Hank Powell lovely? Hank was built like a field plow and was about as lovely as a ball-peen hammer. Only a fag would use such a word.

Then, as if reading poetry or something, he said that West Virginia was full of hollers, twisting roads, and shadows. Just like that. Full of hollers, twisting roads, and shadows. This last word, shadows, he said in an especially strange way. Then he chuckled—I didn't know at what—and had that zigzag smile on his face again.

"Do you know Lisa Kennedy?" I asked.

He made the appearance of thinking about my question.

"She the girl you're looking for?" he asked.

I nodded, and he looked at me for a moment. It was a strange, intrusive look.

"You love her?" he said.

I stared at the ground until he changed the subject and said he needed help with his yard and would pay me to rake it and plant some flowers. When I said nothing to this, he said I could think about it. I said something about my father needing me and headed off into the woods.

That night, I asked my mother if West Virginia was full of shadows. She wasn't sure what I meant, and I couldn't ask it any differently, so I dropped my strange question.

I went back to his house a few days later and stood on his deck until he came to the door and opened it for me. My eyes were full of curiosity as I stepped inside and found myself watching him walk across red carpet. He was older than I thought.

"Willie's been crapping all over the place," he said in a voice I heard as sick and raspy. "Sometimes he gets that way—don't worry, I wouldn't ask you to help me clean that up."

I think he expected me to say something back, but I didn't. Instead, I looked around in triumph. I was the first of my brothers to set foot inside an A-frame. There was no ceiling to speak of, just rafters, and a dead triangular space above them.

On the wall in front of me was a large picture of a boy about my age. He had red hair and a blank expression. I knew immediately—it was one of those moments when my gut was smarter than my head—that it was a sad picture, even though the expression wasn't.

"Bobby," he said, seeing me looking at it. "Bobby Dill." He watched me for a moment, curious of my interest. Then he stepped forward. "He was my neighbor on Cape Cod. Lovely boy. Died of a brain tumor."

It must have been my expression—but he stepped even closer to me. "You're sad today. Why?"

I was always sad, so why did today matter? But I had never been asked why.

"Because of Lisa?" he asked.

I nodded, not even thinking whether it was true or not. I didn't know.

"I know. She was something," he said, as if he knew.

He had in his hand, all this time, a squeezed-up paper towel holding Willie's crap. He asked me to sit, and I did, although he had to point out where, on a baggy chair. He sat, too, on the baggy sofa next to it. He said again, as if a little nervous himself, how much he liked his mountain neighbors. He brought up Hank Powell again.

I said I knew him pretty well.

"A relative?" he asked.

I couldn't tell whether he was serious or not.

"I don't live up here," I said, making this clear. "I'm from Harpers Ferry."

It seemed that this was the first time he heard my voice. His eyes widened. "Oh, well," he said, drawing hard on a cigarette that seemed to appear in his hand by magic. "Anyway, he's a lovely man." He glanced down at Willie lying on the floor. "Fixed that bureau for me." Through the smoke he blew out, he nodded at a desk against the far wall and nodded again until I looked at it.

I looked but didn't really see it. "Lovely" bothered me every time he used it. A man shouldn't use that word. It bothered me also because of all the words, "lovely" was the last I would use to describe any man, particularly Hank Powell. Hank was stout and hard working. Other than that, I didn't know what he was.

"Drives a bus for the county," the old guy went on to say, as if I didn't know.

In the moments after that, we stared so long at each other that I wasn't sure whether his eyes were mine or mine his.

"The mountain culture," he then said, leaning back as if beginning a long story—but then he stopped. He looked straight ahead, his face broken with the smile of someone watching TV and amused by it. He might have sat there for a long while if he hadn't had a cigarette burning between his fingers to snap him out of it. "Tell me about Lisa," he then said that quickly.

I was reluctant at first, and shrugged to show my reluctance, so he mentioned, as if for the sake of talking about girls to a boy like me, that he often saw two girls walking on the road by the store.

I laughed out loud. He was thinking of Pam and Sally. "They're mountain girls," I said, not aware that I was showing disgust.

"Oh, mountain girls," he said. "Pretty, though."

Pretty? He sure had a strange sense of what a pretty girl looked like. For that matter, most of him was strange. As I thought about it, he seemed to view the mountain from high above, from so high above that he couldn't see much up close. He was like the roof of this A-frame, the way it came down sharply, spreading out.

He said he often saw my father delivering mail in Hard Hollow.

I said nothing to this. Instead, I asked him whether he knew Paulie Townsend. To ask him this question was my way of amusing myself with his familiarity with the mountain. He didn't know Paulie by name, but when I described him as the very old man who teetered up and down the same road that Sally and Pam walked, he thought he might have seen him once or twice. He had a faint smile, as if curious of my little diversion.

With my nerve up, I asked him if he were from Cape Cod.

"No," he said right away. He enjoyed stopping me this way, seeing me struggle to say something else. There was a game going on between us, a game of moves. He asked a question. One move. Then I asked my question. Another move. The object of the game, it seemed, was to know the most private things.

He sat for the longest time just looking at me, and I glanced back, each time seeing him still looking at me. We had this manner between us, this manner and method of glancing and staring.

"I've been alone most of my life," he said, out of the blue.

What struck me about this remark was that there seemed to be no strategy to his telling me this, and, naturally, I wondered what his life had been like.

"I've been selfish," he went on, almost as if I had asked him to. "I've had many lovers. Men, women—most haven't been worth it."

I laughed inside at his remark that his lovers hadn't been worth it. Then I felt an excitement at hearing him say "men." It was an excitement like that of being somewhere for the first time. Still, I didn't believe him. I didn't believe for a moment that he had ever had a lover, a woman or a man. I especially couldn't believe that another man would do it with him. He could no more do it than dribble a basketball. He was old, with spindly legs and a big gut and a large, ugly head. He was making it all up.

"Peter was my lover in New Orleans," he said, as if he had had one in every city in America.

Listening to him was like seeing *Playboy* for the first time. You grow up hearing that men could be gay, grow up calling your classmates fags and queers, but until you see one or hear one talk about it, you don't really believe it.

"He loved doing it anywhere, anywhere at all," he went on. "He'd swing from a chandelier."

I felt my mouth about to pop open in laughter. There were other fags in Boatwright Junction, and we teased them, but never got within a mile of them. We had to yell names at them from the hill. But this was an old man who was gay, and it had never occurred to me that an old man could be gay or, for that matter, that a gay man could be old. But here one was, old like my grandfather, though he didn't sound like my grandfather at all. All my grandfather ever talked about was how the railroad was disappearing, how the Orioles were having another bad season, and how much effort it took to grow pumpkins every year.

"You ever want to make it with a man?" he asked.

The question came fast, out of nowhere, but what surprised me was that I didn't feel uncomfortable with it. Actually, I was amused, amused by his angle. I knew what he was and what he doing. He was an old pervert, and he was after me, but he was foolish for thinking

I didn't see through his scheme. He could ask or say whatever he liked. All of this was better than hacking weeds for my father.

I actually felt smug as I sat there thinking about how shocked my parents would be to know what I was hearing. I wondered whether a queer old man had ever said this to my father. The whole time I had that feeling—that feeling of my life being shaken up. I had felt it when I met Lisa, then again when I met Lonny Dunn, the worst roughneck on the mountain, and now this old man.

The longer we sat, the trickier he became. He began comparing us, saying we were the same type of man, sensitive and emotional. Again and again he steered the conversation toward sex. Boys shouldn't have hang-ups about homosexuality, he said, although he said he hated that word, homosexuality. Sounded clinical, he said.

If you put two men together in bed, in the dark, neither, he said, would know the difference. Skin was skin. He made homosexuality sound like a puzzle that could neither be solved nor put down.

Then, that quickly, I could feel it coming—it made me sit slightly out of my body, over the chair and room.

"Come over here," he said with a smile that was slimy and sinister.

I wondered if I would die, be buried under the house like all those kids John Wayne Gacy had killed. I could still run. But I wouldn't. I knew that. I was not the type to run, no matter what he did. He seemed to know that.

As I moved over to the sofa with him, I felt myself sinking into utter submission that was not easy to hide. I could still get away, I told myself. Then, in one great effort with my voice, I asked the only question that came to mind. "Are A-frames hard to heat?"

"Dreadful," he said, believing it was really a question. "Like a fucking church."

I smiled. I liked hearing an adult talk vulgar.

He reached over and started petting my head, and I almost laughed out loud. It seemed I was his dog Willie. I felt his hand run off the sides of my head. I didn't look up at him. He kept saying I was smart and nice-looking. Smart and nice-looking, he said. His breath stunk of tobacco.

Sitting there, I got the feeling, the sick, mixed feeling, that I wasn't as repulsed as I should be.

"See, that's not so bad," he said.

It wasn't, but still it was ridiculous, being petted by an old man like a dog.

He asked me if Lisa ever let me kiss her. I knew he was enjoying this brief trip outside his own experience and into the world of young people. "She let you fuck her?"

I liked hearing him say fuck. I shook my head.

"Just as well," he said, stopping just long enough to light another cigarette with a little green lighter.

I wondered if all fags used little green lighters. For that matter, I wondered if only fags lived in A-frames.

He put the cigarette down, on the edge of the glass table, scooted closer, and slowly he pulled me close to his chest. A hundred thoughts were shooting in different directions. Was I gay? If not, what was wrong with me? What would Lisa think? It took all my strength not to tighten up, to hold my muscles still, as I did not want to show fear. I felt the itchy wool of his sweater and smelled the smoke of his cigarettes. At first, I counted the seconds, waiting for it to be over. Then, before I knew it, I was nearly relaxed.

"There," he said, sitting away from me, "that wasn't too bad, was it?"

I didn't answer.

"Natural enough," he said.

I was unsure of how I felt. The world was blinking and new. To say I was stunned would not be true. To say I enjoyed it wouldn't be, either. It was somewhere in the middle, where I didn't expect it and where I couldn't understand it.

It was late by this time, and he said I should go. He asked when I would be back, and I said tomorrow, although I wasn't so sure. As I walked back through the woods, I felt confused but excited.

The next evening, I hurried back through the woods to see him. As I crossed his yard, I slowed. There was no car in the driveway. He wasn't home. I stood there for a moment without a sense of what to do now. I had counted on seeing him. I had thought about him all day, about the strange, smart things he had said last evening. I was even looking forward to being held again.

I sat on the lounge chair on the deck and looked around, hoping he would see me if he were home. This was River Estates. Lonely this time of week. Not a car on the lane. Just leaves blowing across the deck, the woods thick and still, the faint afternoon sun on the gravel.

I stood and knocked on the door and listened to the dull sound go nowhere inside. Funny that he was all I had to keep myself happy, and I didn't even know him. I tried the doorknob. Locked. I walked around the house, looking in the windows. The sliding glass door on the other side, I discovered, was unlocked. I thought about calling out, but didn't. I stepped in and found myself in the kitchen, where, in the dim light, I started touching everything—counters, walls, vases, edges of picture frames, whatever he owned. I stopped and looked up at the picture Bobby Dill. He looked peaceful in the dim light. Peaceful but dead. I headed down the hallway to the back rooms. The first one I looked into had a film projector in the middle of the floor, along with a roll of Christmas wrapping paper in a corner. I couldn't imagine what he was using that room for. The next was his bedroom. It looked ordinary enough, except for a candy-stripped blanket on the bed. That looked goofy for a man, even though he was gay. I opened a few bureau drawers, and the handles rattled in synch, like brushes against a cymbal. I looked down at his underwear, which were big, baggy, and not so white anymore. Farther down the hall there was another room, but it was too dark to see in, and I couldn't find the light switch.

I felt nervous suddenly and hurried back to the living room, where I noticed his telephone. It was a trim white phone, the kind used in businesses, and was placed neatly on a glass table. I picked it up and put it to my ear and listened to its strong dial tone. I admired all the lighted buttons, touched one, and it beeped at me. I wished I had someone to call, someone who would be full of curiosity, wanting to know where I was calling from. From a nice house in River Estates, I would say. An A-frame. I would describe it as being cool and weird, shaped like a long teepee with straight sides, having air-conditioning, new furniture, and carpeting.

Then, in a flash, the living room light came on around me. When I looked up, Carter was standing halfway in the front door, his hand on the light switch. If he were startled, he didn't show it.

"What are you doing?"

All I could do was stand up.

"How'd you get in?"

This question he wanted me to answer. So I told him. He stood looking at me, trying to decide, I could tell, what he should do now, having found me in his house. He pushed the door shut.

"Who were you calling?"

I told him the truth. No one.

He was looking down at the red carpeting as he made his way around the sofa toward me, where he dropped his keys on the coffee table.

"I'm not angry," he said. As he said this, his dog Willie came from behind him, trotted up to me, and looked me straight in the face. "Yes, Willie, we have a surprise visitor," he said.

I was angry, though, angry that he had sneaked up on me and angry that I had let myself be sneaked up on. Angry, too, that I was so helpless. As I looked at him, he could have been thinking anything.

"Let's go to the bedroom," he said just like that.

I stood frozen for a moment, then headed down the hall.

"This doesn't mean you're gay," he said as I walked ahead of him.

No? Then what did it mean? It didn't mean I was normal either. If I was ugly, then that was why. But when I looked at myself in the mirror, I didn't think I was ugly, maybe a little soft-faced here and there, even girlish around the eyes, but not plain ugly. Still, since this was happening, Lisa must have been a fluke. Pam, too.

Maybe I talked about my feelings too much to girls. Sounded icky, like a little boy. I was that way with Lisa in my letters.

I sat on the bed as he told me, and he did not switch on the light. Just the light from the hallway came in. He did not waste time. I felt his hand on my leg, and it was working its way up. Strange, but I did not feel violated—in some way I understood his need. I had my own for Lisa.

But I was angry with my penis for getting hard, as if a person could be angry with his penis. How could it do such a thing? How could it make me feel gay?

I did not hate him—I hated Lisa. I hated her for leaving me this way, so lonely and mixed up, so pathetic that I was lying in a bed with an old man. I understood what she had said about the importance of being with the right person the first time.

"Jason, I can feel your penis," she had said the one time I tried to get close to her, as if my penis was something horrible. She said it went against the church.

"Why is Hank lovely?" I asked him. I was desperate to distract him. Anything to keep him thinking. To keep his mind off me. But he told me to be quiet, though not in a mean way.

I looked out the window at the stars. Even if she was looking up at them right now, she could never imagine the mess I was in, what I was doing to myself. We were truly apart now.

But she would care if she knew; she would care even if she no longer loved me. She would be concerned that I was doing the wrong thing to myself. But she still would not love me. Knowing that was the worst part about lying in bed with him.

"This is nice," he said in a sleepy, happy voice.

I could kill him, I thought. Beat him to death with something. A vase. An old man! This was the best I could do? A queer old man?

"Did Lisa ever do this to you?" he asked, putting his hand right over the spot.

No, I said, hating the fact that I had to answer. It was hard, and I was angry at the same time.

"Little priss," he said.

For a brief moment, I almost laughed. She was a little priss. As if he knew her, she was a little priss.

With his hand resting there, he went on to say some foul things about women, that basically they couldn't be trusted, although he used much worse words. Then, suddenly, he sat up and got off the bed.

I sat up, too, as if we should do everything together now, as though we were a couple or something disgusting like that. And I followed him down the hall, too, almost out of reaction, as if someone had kicked me in the knee or something, making my leg pop up. I saw nothing of what was around me. My head was a whirl of thoughts.

In the living room, he lit his cigarette, then looked at me in the baggy TV chair, which was becoming my chair. He said I could help myself to anything in the refrigerator. But I wasn't moving.

Everything was crazy. Him being gay and touching me. I wanted to be angry, but for some reason wasn't. He leaned forward and tapped his cigarette against a light-filled brown glass ashtray that reminded me of the bottles in my grandmother's liquor store, then sat back and trained his eyes on me once again.

". . . lest the unwelcome child be exposed to any fate," he said.

I knew he was reading from some book in his head. His mouth had a million words in there, and they popped out in all different combinations. I could not imagine him a preacher of any kind, and he was too dirty-mouthed to be a teacher either.

"Did you study religion in college?"

It was the most intelligent-sounding question I could come up with.

"No," he said.

For a moment I thought that was all he would say, that we were back to our game, one-word moves at a time.

"Interior decorating."

I had little idea of what that was, other than the obvious, and looked around at his furniture as if to consider his work. There were nifty, fat chairs, skinny lamps, bright carpeting, but you didn't seem to need a college degree to put that together. What stood out, I thought, were his stereo speakers, covered in a patchwork denim. It looked like scraps from ten different pairs of faded blue jeans.

I looked at him for a while. Always the looking. That was our way. Eye contact.

I asked again why Hank was "lovely." I listened to myself using this word. The world did not crack open. I did not grow breasts.

He looked off as if to consider my question. I liked this about him, that he took my questions seriously. He kept looking off and thinking.

"Because," he said, tapping his cigarette, "he's quiet, considerate."

It was a disappointing answer, though, after all the wonder I had over it. I still wasn't sure if I was understanding his words the way he meant them.

"I'll tell you why I like this area, Jason," he said.

I looked over at him.

"It's lonelier than me, and I feel safe here in that way."

I didn't understand the remark, but I took notice that he called himself lonely.

"The mountain's lonely," I said.

"Is it?" he said.

I hated when he did this. Now I had to explain myself from the start.

"My father makes it lonely," I said, trying to take a shortcut.

"Yeah," he said, looking away, "he's a real pisser."

I didn't know what that word meant, but I could guess by the sound of it.

"Have you ever been with a woman?" I asked.

"Oh sure," he said.

He liked this question, as if he thought it made us close.

Long, sharp shadows angled across his light blue shirt, and his green and yellow golfer's pants he wore were completely in shadow. He told me about a woman he had lived with for eleven years on Cape Cod, an older woman he had taken care of.

"One morning, I woke, and could tell she was dead. Something about the light in the room, the feel of the house. Didn't even check her room, just called her doctor."

He wanted my curiosity, and he had it. His past was like something out of a book. When he then told me he had been an alcoholic for twenty years, I found it hard to believe. There were alcoholics on my father's side of the family, and they lived in trailers and every Friday stumbled down Route 340 to the VA hospital for something free. But he had a nice house and a new car. Still, he said he had lived at home with his mother until his early thirties. She used to come into his room where he was hung over late in the morning and say, "Get up out of that," meaning the bed. He hated the way she said "that."

He found himself nearly forty, drunk and unemployed, when he joined the park service for the sole purpose of earning a pension. The secret of success, he said, was being a good bullshitter. He said he used to read the dictionary for fun and he knew too many words for his own good. When he was trying to get his start in advertising, he sent his resume out printed in white ink on blue paper, to get attention.

He put out his cigarette and lit another one. "Now, tell me something interesting," he said. That was our deal. He told me something personal and private, then I did.

I sat looking down at the floor.

"I know," he said after a moment. "I know what you're thinking."

I looked up.

"It doesn't mean you're a fag, okay?"

I nodded, even though I didn't really believe what he said.

We sat quietly for a moment longer, glancing at each other.

"I did that back there," he said, jabbing his thumb toward the rear of the house, "to establish trust."

I told myself I understood, tried to, but didn't entirely. Still I nodded. It was the thing to do at the moment.

When he spoke of growing up in the Bronx, in a time when his

Italian and Irish neighbors were "industrious," I began to think differently of him, knowing now that there was a tough guy in him. Even so, he was still toughest on himself. He was selfish, he said. Competitive, manipulative, he went on. As far as his homosexuality, he seemed to blame it on an incident that happened to him. He gave no time or place, but I got the feeling it occurred in Oklahoma, where he said he had run a furniture store. He was picked up by the police for having an expired driver's license and, at the police station, was raped.

"I didn't mind really," he said, "but he damaged my rectum."

After that, he was gay, or so he seemed to say.

I sat there, fascinated. The most exciting story my grandfather had to tell was when the bird feeder fell on his head.

He talked about being a second lieutenant in the army, too, in charge of an all-black infantry unit. They were frightened of him, he said, because his face turned bright red in the sun and his hair was as yellow as corn silk.

When he then told me he had gone to the Boston School of Art and graduated with a degree in interior design, it seemed he was mixing adventures he had read about. I wondered where he had found the time to be a nurse for an elderly woman, a drunk living with his mother, a furniture store manager in Oklahoma, a park ranger on Cape Cod, in advertising, a second lieutenant in the army, and an art student in Boston, all at the same time, it seemed. Add to that his love affair with Peter in New Orleans. Not that I ever really thought he was lying. But when it came to his life, I just had no sense of a timeline.

"I can remember the first time I saw this area," he said.

He had been driving down from Cape Cod when he saw the mountains just outside Frederick. It was a stunning sight, he said.

I looked over at his grainy, red-complected face and wondered how it was in the world I was coming to be friends with him. I felt I was learning something new and having my feelings straightened out along the way. That was why we were friends. He was eccentric, and I was his candidate for something.

"When I was in art school in Boston," he said, "everybody came to me for ideas. I was the idea man." He looked off. "Just as well."

He lit another cigarette, and the flick of his lighter was a kind of signal to begin something new. He was patient as he looked at me, puffed, but said nothing.

Indians and Teddy Bears Were Here First

***

I leafed through the Nakakoji Land Development brochure until coming to "Welcome to Sunrise Hills" in big cloud-like letters floating through fancy English Tudor windows that were open to a view of the Blue Ridge Mountains in autumn.

"*Wow*," I couldn't help but say aloud in the school's library.

Set amidst the Blue Ridge Mountains of West Virginia and encompassing more than 1,000 acres with thirty-six holes of championship golf, six tennis courts, skiing, swimming, fishing, and more—all just fifty-eight miles from the nation's capital and minutes away from historic Harpers Ferry. Homesites from $135,000; homes from $229,000.

So this was where my grandfather lived now?

With an amazed grin, I headed down the hall to the school's bulletin board. There were typed-up editorials posted everywhere about the school protest, mostly that everyone should be suing the cops for brutality. I started reading them.

```
. . . I'm suspicious. Whoever found Bolívar's bayonet
is probably being paid to keep silent. I'm guessing one of
its own—a park archaeologist . . .

        . . . fellow sleuths. Here's my take. "Raiders of the
Lost Ark" or "X-Files" . . . another historical artifact,
like the Ark of the Covenant recovered from the Temple in
Jerusalem, has been locked in a crate and put in a giant
warehouse somewhere in Harpers Ferry, never to be seen
again—all to ensure that no history books will have to be
rewritten and that no history professor will have to revise
the lecture that he has been giving for the last 140 years
. . .
```

I read a few more, then hurried to class. At 3:50, when Severe St. Cyr finally let us go, assigning twenty pages of French by tomorrow, I made a beeline for Granddad's gated community. In my heart I had a special kind of invitation: the school protest. It was just the kind of rebellious event I was sure he'd admire.

I hadn't seen Granddad in a full year, and, honestly, until now, I doubted that he would have wanted to see me again. After Grandma died last year, Mom tried to make me into his teddy bear or something—you know, be a cute kid for him to watch baseball games with, make him all happy again. At the time, he was in a club of the worst kind, the Harpers Ferry widower's club—short, old Irish men with bad knees who wore the same brown slacks everyday and stood out on the sidewalk as if not sure which house was theirs. Everyone expected him to die of grief and loneliness. We watched a few Orioles games together. He told me to do well in school. I even mowed his lawn.

Then, not long after, he went off the deep end. He traded in his old car for a flashy new one and took half a dozen trips to

Florida. With Grandma, the farthest he had ever gone was twenty-two miles to Berryville, Virginia, for the Apple Blossom Parade. He started wearing tight white pants, behaving like a man half his age. He even sold the treasured old Harpers Ferry house he and Grandma had lived in for forty years and moved—not saying where for the longest while. Mom said good riddance. She thought he was perfectly ridiculous.

Secretly, I thought he was cool for finally getting a life. With Grandma, he had been a boring husband. All he ever did was drive her to the Women's Club every Thursday. The rest of the time he sat in his air-conditioned living room and played around with his RCA TV. He even kept a bird feeder. Dad said that was the problem with men who raised only daughters.

Then, last week, Mom told me Granddad was back in the area, living in Sunrise Hills. So, today, with some extra time after school, I decided to check out where he lived. I could find anyone in this town. Honestly, I couldn't wait to see him again, to see how different he had become. Telling him about the student protest was the perfect excuse.

Walking down Washington Street, I passed the oldest Harpers Ferry houses. All had big names. Our Lady of Longstreet was a yellow mansion with curvy white columns. McClellan's Charge and Burnside's Brigade were not imposing structures, but actually adorable brick bungalows with white candles in the windows.

Exactly at the Bolivar town limits, the red, white, and blue center lines that were the pride of Harpers Ferry ended, and the road continued on, unlined and cracked up. The sidewalk stopped, too, replaced by a weedy shoulder littered with junk cars and broken glass. Years ago, someone had spray-painted "Eat me" across the Entering Bolivar sign, but the Leaving Bolivar sign across the road, they left alone. That one was joke enough.

"Leaving Bolivar," it read. "*Please* come back!" Harpers Ferrians still howled about that.

Following the map, deeper and deeper into Bolivar I went, past pool halls with busted up Coke machines in front and a tavern called The Little Brown Jug. Shirtless black kids were out on every corner, gawking at the whitey coming through.

At Tarton Street, buildings were nothing but cinderblock shells. What stoplights there were, were blinking red. Graffiti was every-where—on telephone poles, dilapidated porches. Window fronts were black and cruddy, doors boarded up. Tops of parking meters were missing. Yellowed newspapers lay on the walk.

I came to a stop, looking down at the map. This couldn't be right. I must have screwed up.

Ahead stood Senator Byrd's new roadside sign that read, "Federal Restoration Project. History of Old Bolivar Campaign. *Please donate your time.*" There was even a smiley face underneath.

I turned left, past a burnt-out laundry van, then right, down a dirt street full of little aluminum-siding houses every shade of blue and gray.

I followed the street to the tee, but somewhere on River Street, I managed to get completely lost. Dogs were barking all around me, and overhead was the sizzle of sagging power lines, like black snakes frying on the sky. I ended up cutting through weedy lots, crossing patches of woods, and roaming down pig paths full of beer can tabs. Where in the hell was I? Granddad would never live around here.

I went farther than I thought I should, over a concrete bridge without guard rails, to a potholed area of street. To get my bearings, I tromped out into an open field, my sneaker laces picking up thistle burrs. Then, over the rise, I came to a stop as if having walked up on a flying saucer. Just past the drooping mulberry trees was an incredible sight—emerald-green grass to the horizon, new asphalt streets the color of chocolate, and a hundred little red roofs pitched sharply against the sky. A brand-new, perfect little town!

I ran forward into a little park in the community. There were picnic tables the color of my father's good oxblood shoes, slides as shiny as bumpers, and bright-orange rocking horses mounted to the ground by truck springs painted baby-blue. There was even an old-time bandstand with an American flag over it—all surrounded by a chain-link fence shimmering a diamond wire pattern high and wide enough to keep out King Kong.

"This is it!" I said to myself, spinning around.

Somehow I had taken the worst streets here, but this was definitely it.

"Sunrise Hills," it said on a big sign off to the right. "Private Community." I had to say the words aloud. "*Private Community?*"

Nearby was a smaller sign. "Premium Lakefront Home Sites. Tours by appointment/reservation only."

Shit, this is nicer than Harpers Ferry! I thought. Tennis court, golf course, lake—he's rich! I could hear my mother popping out her miserable laugh.

I jogged along the shiny chain-link fence until I came to the security kiosk, where a potbellied guard leaned out. He seemed to remember me, or thought he knew me. He pointed down over the hill toward the lake. My grandfather, he told me, was at the café by the caddie cars. Stay off the grass, he added.

As I passed through the main gate, I felt I'd entered a futuristic world. Spotless grass. Trees that looked cloned. No broken glass on the street. It was a night and day difference compared to the old houses on Tarton Street. Made me wonder who would put a private community so close to the worst houses around, where it would gloat about its money and not care how bad off anyone else was.

I wandered around the parking lots filled with new cars, most with Maryland and Virginia plates. There were no signs of black people in here, no plastic crucifixes over the mirrors, no Pampers on front seats, no fishing poles in back. These Audis and Toyotas were spotless, many with colorful kayaks on the roof, beachballs, and baby strollers in the backseat.

Finally I came upon a red sportscar with a personalized license plate—REBORN. I peered through the back window. Just a clothes hanger hooked above the backseat window. In the glass I saw the reflection of a man looking down at me from the porch above. I whirled around—Granddad!

I hardly recognized him, he looked so different. Wearing a pumpkin-colored shirt and khaki-tan shorts, he looked like a tourist from the KOA campground.

"Well, hello," he said, standing up straight over a planter of red flowers and smiling. "I see you found me." He glanced around the cars behind me. "Your brother with you?"

When I shook my head, he waved me up the patio steps. I charged up, running into a lady wearing a belt so tight it squeezed her middle thin like an ant's.

"Monica," Granddad said, putting down a nifty green sprinkler bucket, "this is one of Katie's boys."

I drew back into infinity. Granddad had a "friend." She stood there as if she owned not only the porch but the whole community as well, smiling with perfect fake teeth. She said hello in a dry, fancy voice. All the while, a car alarm was going off in my mind. *Granddad has a girlfriend! Granddad has a girlfriend! Granddad has a girlfriend!*

He went into hospitality mode, and we all sat at an iron table under a big yellow umbrella. Granddad had apparently outgrown his spandex phase; he was wearing cargo shorts, which hung down his short legs like saddlebags. He had on a sporty black wristwatch and wire-frame glasses that made him look retired and rich. All the years he had been married to Grandma, he never wore anything other than brown slacks and Arrow shirts. He had lost weight, too, and if he was still limping, I sure didn't see it. Some of his hair had grown back, too. Life inside this fence, with this woman, had made him younger. He looked like Theodore Roosevelt with one of "The Golden Girls."

"I was just reading about your classmates," he said, nodding at a newspaper on the table.

When I caught sight of "Protesting Students" in the headline, I sat up and jabbed my thumb against my chest. "I was in it!"

"Oh, *you* were in it?" he said back, getting excited, too.

He looked over at this woman. I sat nodding my head off. And just like that, it seemed I was in his good graces.

"But *have* you seen this article, dear?" asked this woman.

Her voice was every kid's nightmare. It had the quintessential nasally, disapproving sound of a librarian. Granddad slid the *Bolivar Bugle* under my nose.

Protesting Students Miss the Point of Bolívar's Bayonet

HARPERS FERRY, WV. (June 3) Harpers Ferry police and mounted park rangers dispersed a crowd of student protesters Friday on the historic streets of Harpers Ferry. Several cases of vandalism—

I glanced up at Granddad. Vandalism? There was no vandalism. I swear. He sat giving me a look that I couldn't easily read. Not disapproval exactly. Not admiration either. I read on.

—there were no arrests, however, and only one minor injury was reported.

Dozens of Harpers Ferry High students took part in the protest calling for the town to change its name to Bolivar and be incorporated into the neighboring town by the same name, in light of a recent historical find some say challenges the validity of historical accounts of the region. Last May, a socket-type bayonet reportedly containing Simón Bolívar's seal was uncovered by park authorities, throwing into question the town's historical bragging rights—the American Civil War or Bolívar's South American war of liberation? Simón Bolívar, nicknamed "George Washington of South America," is renowned for leading bloody revolts against Spanish authority in Venezuela, Peru, and Bolivia in the early 1800s. Bolivar, West Virginia, ranks as one of the state's poorest towns.

Friday's protest took place on historic High Street in front of scores of landmark scenic homes. Students blocked holiday traffic, cheering and waving banners, in a sixties style sit-in that lasted some four hours and drew media attention as far away as Frederick, Maryland. Park authorities said the interruption, which caused only minor traffic jams in the historic town, had no lasting effect on tourism on the first weekend of summer. An estimated one million tourists visit the lower town each summer.

According to Harpers Ferry High principal Walter Higgins, the purpose of the gathering was to encourage school spirit in civic action. A petition calling for a referendum has collected nearly three hundred signatures, he said.

"If this was some sort of civics lesson, they missed the point," said Harpers Ferry third-term Mayor Alexander Baxtor. "This kind of behavior sends the wrong message to the town's youth—that change can be demanded."

I sat stunned. They were out of their minds. We had done a good thing—no, a great thing! What could be better than knocking Harpers Ferry richees down a peg?

Granddad, putting the newspaper aside, tried to make light of the moment. He asked about school, home, and my mother, and I kept the answers simple. All the while, a big worry was flashing in my mind—what vandalism? No one had gotten out of hand, unless Gregg or Corn Puff had done something. What would Granddad think of me now?

As I looked down at the fancy ice tea glasses, then around at the hundreds upon hundreds of yards of spotless green grass set against the blue mountains, gone was feeling of this being a perfect place. Instead, it felt like we were sitting on an Indian burial ground or something.

Soon Granddad ran out of small-talk, and he and Monica passed glances.

"You know, I'm surprised they let you in," he said. "They're usually pretty good about that." He looked over at her. "*All visitors must be announced.* That's what the sign says."

She reached across the small table and, with a fancy paper napkin with lettering on it, wiped up the water ring left by my glass.

"Well, they should be pretty good about it," she said, dabbing the spot dry. "We pay them enough."

She had perfect older skin and bright-red fingernails. I wondered if she was a rich widow. Finally, Granddad cleared his throat and gave me a furrowed look.

"Son, did your mother ask you to come here for some reason?"

"Oh, now Roy," Monica said, with a big phony smile, "Katie would never do that."

She tapped him on the hand, then asked me how my mother was, sounding as if she knew her—knew her well. I said fine, for the second or third time. She took over the conversation from this point on, saying she didn't know how my mother managed three boys where we lived, surrounded by all those tourists. My mother should move up the hill, she said, to one of those quiet backstreets. Katie should do this, Katie should do that. All the while, Granddad sat quietly.

Then we all started inside, with Granddad holding the door for me. He and I sat on a bright, flowery sofa, and Monica on a TV chair made of black leather. Above her on a shelf was a strange lizard figurine with a head as a water sprinkler. Beside it was a small cactus. On the walls were sailing pictures and paintings of clowns. There was a coffee table made entirely of green glass and a vanity mirror curved like a woman. Except for the wind chimes outside, I didn't see one thing from his old house. No heavy-framed, old pictures of Grandma, no chipped antiques, and no rolling ball clock.

"I tell you what's got me worried," Granddad said, keeping the conversation on the Orioles. "The outfield. Without Castleberry, they've got no speed."

"They can always move Lowenstein over to center and put Williams in right," I said, watching Monica get up.

As she stepped past me toward the kitchen, I couldn't help but look at her figure. She was smaller than my mother, but wore a belt as wide as my brother's weight-lifting belt. Red and glossy, it looked like a bow around her middle. Grandma had been at least twice as fat and would have never worn hula hoop earrings.

"Jason," she said from the refrigerator, "Roy tells me you want to be an artist."

"That reminds me," Granddad said. "You should talk to your counselor about scholarships."

"She said wait till my junior year."

"Wait until your junior year?" he said. "That's ridiculous."

Out of the corner of my eye, I watched Monica wheel out a fancy cart full of the tiniest, diamond-shaped sandwiches. As Granddad and I made room for the cart, she told me she had once dabbled in pastels herself. She had a voice that made me think of a boarding school. I could also tell she wasn't from Jefferson County just by the way she wheeled the little cart. She made it do all the work.

Granddad, meanwhile, went on shaking his head over my counselor, grumbling that this wait-and-do-nothing attitude was typical of people around here.

"Son," he said finally, "we've got to get you out of this place."

Monica looked at the side of his head as if there was a gaping hole in it.

"Why, Roy?"

He turned to her. "Well, he's not like his brothers, dear."

"I know, but where?" she asked. "He can't just go anywhere." Her smile turned awful-looking. "I mean, he's grown up here."

"Corcoran School of Art & Design," I started spelling out for her, too. "500 Seventeenth Street, NW, Washington, DC, 20004 . . . "

Granddad, after giving me a blank look, said to her, "Well, I grew up here, too, dear."

"But *you*, dear," she said toward his ear, as if he was hard of hearing, "didn't leave."

In that instant, I knew everything. I knew that this condo was hers, that she had all the money, and that she was in charge. I even knew why he never loved Grandma, as Mom said it, or at least why he had always been so quiet around her. His life, even after Grandma, was still on hold.

Monica, meanwhile, went on about how hard it would be for me "adjusting" to living in D.C., that it would be a lonely place. She reminded me that my family was from here. She used the word heritage. This was my heritage, she said.

"Why?" she asked me again. "Why do you want to go there, Jason?"

Why? No one asked why. But she didn't sound like my father who spoke out of fear. She sounded worse—smart.

"I think maybe your counselor's right," she said. "You should wait until you get a better idea of what—"

"No, no," said Granddad, pulling his chair up to the table, "he should plan."

"*Plan*, yes," she said back, shaking her head, "but I just don't think we should be giving anybody any *unrealistic expectations.*"

She said this like the name of a book. When she asked me when I had been to D.C. last and I said five years ago, in the fourth grade, back came her awful smile. It had a definite way of putting me down, despite the pink sandwich guck between her teeth. Not that she had pink sandwich guck between her teeth, but it had a definite way of putting me down.

"You two make it sound like this is some horrible place," she said, putting her sandwich down.

You better believe it was horrible. She just didn't understand. She had this attitude that all of Harpers Ferry was *so* charming and quaint, with its pretty little shops and grand views. She sounded just like a tourist. She was obviously sheltered back here in this fancy place.

"What about schools around here?" she said. "They have a good art program at Longwood. That would be more realistic."

Longwood Smongwood! My stupid art teacher had gone there and wanted all his students to follow in his footsteps. I was better than a stupid West Virginia teacher's college.

"Why don't you get a summer job at one of the museums here in town first?" she went on.

The woman wouldn't stop.

"Young man, you're living in one of the most historically rich, scenic areas of the country—I mean, as an artist, I would think you would flourish here!"

I hated her. We sat eating quietly. The ham spread had no taste, the bread was stale, and the iced tea was warm. I put my food back on the plate—I had lost my appetite—and went back to looking around the room. Acrylic rugs. Lavender curtains. Lots of what Mom would call imitation-wood furniture. Granddad was living like a mousy yuppie.

Monica, having calmed down, helped herself to another bite-sized sandwich, then wiped her lips with her pinky, which she held out as if to have fitted with a diamond ring.

"Roy—hmm, I think I put in too much dill—do you remember that time—" She stopped, looked over at me, and, suddenly pretending to be friendly, asked me if I at least enjoyed my art class up at the high school, if I had a good teacher, and if he taught watercolors.

"He's okay," I mumbled.

"Just okay?"

"He's too easy now. Paint by numbers stuff."

I was just trying to get through the rest of the visit. But I only made things worse again when I said Mr. Thompson had never been out of West Virginia, and I could hear myself trying to sound like a big-shot when I said he had never seen van Gogh's *Gardens of the Sunlight* or Picasso's *The Tragedy* at the National Gallery of Art.

"Van Gogh himself," she said right back, "never saw a city until he was twenty-eight."

"Is that right?" Granddad said, trying to make us all agreeable now.

Monica nodded a superior little nod.

"Well, I guess it doesn't matter with art," he said.

She kept looking at me. And the sorer I felt, the more she

looked. She hated me, and the feeling was mutual. When she asked me if I drew every day, I said no. When she asked me if I carried a sketchpad everywhere I went, I was forced to say no again. When she asked me if I kept a journal, read art magazines, talked to local artists, I was beginning to feel taken apart.

"Why the rush, Jason?" she finally asked.

I'd never answer her now, even if she were the last person on earth.

"Because, Monica, dear," Granddad said, "he doesn't want to end up like me."

Suddenly, she was full of apology. When she bent down to kiss his bald head, I looked away. Granddad won the argument for both of us, but at his own expense.

Minutes later, when he walked me outside, he was all smiles and said that Monica was just playing Devil's advocate. She was the devil all right.

"So," he said, heading me over to the picnic tables, which was the same as escorting me off the grounds, "who do you think was here first—Simón Bolívar or John Brown? It's in all the papers."

I looked at him, daring him to speak of what really mattered. It wasn't this fancy show-off place he was living in, right in the face of all the poor blacks. It wasn't that Mom had disowned him for having a girlfriend now at seventy, after having been married to Grandma for a hundred years. It wasn't even that he had picked a critical, snooty, and condescending lady. How could he talk to me about life or the city? It was that, after a year, *I* had to come and find him. He had left me behind like a worn-out teddy bear.

"The Indians," I said, walking on toward the gate by myself. "The Indians were here first."

The

Scratchboard Project

***

"Draw Shanice?" Mrs. Sharpe said through the screen door, wiping her hands on a towel. She glanced down at the sketchpad under my arm. Behind her, shirtless little black kids were hopping around. They opened the screen door themselves and flooded around me on the porch.

"Everyone, this is Jason."

They looked up, and in that instant, as I looked down at all of them, I saw for the first time the world in X-ray—black and white shapes floating before my eyes like objects tied to a mobile, just as my art teacher Mr. Thompson wanted us to see for the scratchboard project.

The scratchboard project. An exercise in negative and positive relationships. You started with a piece of board with black coating on it, and you had to take your etcher and etch out a drawing, make a white image out of solid blackness. Essentially, you had to draw in reverse. You left black what you ordinarily drew in and took away what you ordinarily left white.

The rules for the project were simple: pick someone in school you don't know; go to their house and study them "gesturally"; then turn them inside out, through sketches later to be used as templates for transfer to the scratchboard.

Naturally I had procrastinated, and now everybody I halfway knew from every decent house in town had been taken. I ended up here, in the next town, Bolivar, on this god-forsaken porch. Shanice Sharpe was the meanest black militant bitch in school. Her little brothers stood gazing up at me with placid faces that I was sure would turn inside out and hiss like demons.

Mrs. Sharpe shooed them away from my legs.

"Jason is in Shani's grade in school," she said. "He lives over in *Happers* Ferry."

"Alabama?" said the littlest one.

She led me inside to a small, dark room crowded with junk I couldn't see well. Chairs, boxes, and bags of aluminum cans—all were in our way, along with stacks of *Washington Post* TV guides. There were SONY TV boxes used as furniture, holding up gigantic boxes of Cheerios and Pampers. On the walls were so many pictures of black children with shining white teeth that I couldn't see what was underneath—wood, mud, straw, or aluminum siding with bullet holes. There were crucifixes, too, not the good Irish Catholic kind, but cheap-looking white plastic ones, from a five-and-ten somewhere.

All the kids were yapping at once. Shanice's brother Tyrone came out of nowhere. He was so enormous he had to lower his head under the doorway. He had on sneakers that were as big as snowshoes, an orange tank top that came down to his knees like a dress, and cap turned backward. The sight of me standing in his house took him by surprise, and he stood there shyly.

"Tyrone, you wanna show Jason your trophy?" she said, speaking to us like a kindergarten teacher. "Go on now."

I followed him into an even smaller room. Nintendo games on the floor, posters of black girls in bikinis all over the place.

"Here," he said, his big arm swinging around.

All I saw were greasy black fingers around a shiny silver trophy that looked stolen. I had to say something.

"You won that?"

He turned around and stood up against me. I barely came up to the zero on his jersey.

"Yeah, I won that. What'd you think? Came in a box of Cheerios?"

Truthfully, yeah. He might have had me alone, but I wasn't as scared of him as he thought, even if he was three times bigger.

"Where you live in *Happers* Ferry, little man? Ridge Street?"

"Polk Street," I said.

"Pork who?" He broke into a stupid snicker, his shiny black face all scrunched up. "Shit, Jed Clampett Jr."

Then he asked me something in black gibberish, but I didn't understand and stood staring back at him.

"Damn, dude," he said, coming in clear now and flipping his big hands around like a Magic Johnson or something, "you want a Coke or not?"

Mrs. Sharpe, appearing at the door, looked concerned.

"Tyrone," she said, "remember what we talked about?"

He went into his big shy kid routine, plopping his huge body down on a spring bed, squeaking it to death.

"Yes, ma'am, my manners."

He was so shame-faced and meek, beaten down by his mother, that I didn't know who was worse off—him or me.

"Jason is just shy," Mrs. Sharpe said.

No, I wasn't. I had just trapped myself in this filthy Bolivar house, with all these black kids staring at me and God only knows what heaped around me—guns, drugs. All for the stupid scratch-board project, the biggest damn worry in my life.

Mr. Thompson was making it a whopping 50 percent of our grade, and if I failed art—and I was already failing French—then I'd fail two classes, and maybe the whole year as a result. How could I even be in this situation? No one in my family had ever been held back a year.

Mr. Thompson said:

- Think in terms of negative and positive space,
- Take things apart. See your environment differently.
- Learn to observe, rather than working from memory.

Pure torture. Nobody did scratchboard today. It went out with cave painting. If not then, with sixteenth-century printmaking. It was impossible to think in reverse for very long. Sooner or later you etched away too much black coating, and you were sunk. But there was no adding back, not like drawing with a pencil, when all you did was add.

But here I was in the worst house in Bolivar, with a tribe of blacks gawking and laughing at me, armed with only a sketchpad. It all seemed a weird dream, like Jason in Africa or something.

To find a place to put my eyes, I looked around at the walls. I saw the negative and positive shapes reversing—the dark book shelf becoming light, the light wall becoming dark, the whole X-ray effect again. Suddenly, out of a cubbyhole in this house appeared a girl who looked like a black Barbie doll. Makeup, earrings, Donna Summer hairdo. She was so pretty she looked stolen, like the TV set and Tyrone's silver trophy. Shanice! She looked so different I hadn't recognized her. In school, she always wore a scarf or hand-kerchief over her head. She saw me and went into nasty mode.

"What's he doing here?"

Her thin eyebrows were raised up like daggers.

"To see you," said her brother, rolling on the springy bed, enjoying every bit of his little joke. He was just like my brother Andy—a menace.

Then, all eyes fell on me again and my sketchpad.

"Jason is here for a school project," Mrs. Sharpe told the little ones, trying to keep the situation under control. "To draw your sister."

"I know," said Shanice. "He a show-off, too."

"I'm an artist," Tyrone said, sitting up.

He took off his cap to show me letters shaved into his afro in back, but I couldn't make out what they spelled.

"Damn, he dumb," said Shanice.

I gave her a look. She might have made herself as pretty as a model, but she was still trash on the inside.

"Jason, does your mother know you're here?" Mrs. Sharpe asked me.

I nodded, and she smiled.

"She works for the town, doesn't she?"

Technically, it was for the mayor.

"They live in that big rich place with all them limos around it," said Tyrone, daring me to deny it.

He was referring to Robert Byrd's house on Ridge Street. All the little kids' eyes went wide.

"You rich?" said one of them, pulling on my finger.

Shanice was in no mood for all this chummy talk. She crossed her arms and nodded at me. "Why you here?"

"He wants to draw you," said her mother. "For a school project."

I couldn't understand Mrs. Sharpe's kindness. Her face had all the torture of slaves in paintings down in the Harpers Ferry Visitor's Center, but she went on being kind like my mother, who looked like Sandy Duncan.

"Draw me?" said Shani.

"I know what he want," said Tyrone, snickering.

"He rich," said the same little boy.

"You here to fix our step?" said another.

I kept my eyes on Mrs. Sharpe. She was my only hope.

Just then, a little fat-faced girl pushed her way in close. "Shanice think you cute," she said.

Tyrone kicked his big foot at her, then tossed his yellow notebook at me.

"Don't *look* at me, Jed," he said, with another rapper's wiggle of his hands. "*Draw* me, brother."

He earned a few laughs for his antic.

But when I slid the chair around to see him straight on, everyone knew I meant business. Maybe I couldn't draw in reverse, but drawing regular—now that was something I could do. I opened my sketchpad, but Tyrone said he wanted the drawing in his notebook. That way he could keep it to show everyone. Mrs. Sharpe was looking on intently. I was like Father Flanagan and the kids were like orphans as they gathered around, clinging to my shoulders and legs and breathing in my ear. One of the little ones was actually lying across my knee. It was the strangest feeling. In seconds, I had gone from a white boy to hate to someone with magic in his fingers.

I had never drawn a black face before, except from a painting of John Henry. Not that it mattered. In portraits, every face was different. As Mr. Thompson put it, each feature was a certain distance away from the other, an exact position and relation. There were basic guideposts to follow: Between the eyes, leave space for a third eye. For the nose, start with the crescents of the nostrils. Also, remember to line the center of the mouth up with the bottom of the ears. I liked to think of it as plotting stars. Everyone's eyes, nose, and lips were like stars making up a constellation: Big Dipper, Southern Cross, Canis Minor. The kind of paper didn't matter, and a pencil was a pencil, as long as it could be made either dark or light.

Tyrone's notebook was how I imagined his locker—full of doodles and stupid words like "bitch rammer'" and "funk train"—the work of a seven-foot third-grader gone delinquent. I unjammed his chewed-up pencil from the spiral binding and put the notebook square on my lap. Tyrone, arms folded and big legs coming off the bed like toppled telephone poles, gave me a smug, sweaty stare. I went into my drawing mode, gazing at him for a long moment, seeing him only as the subject, not worrying about him as the big bully he was.

"You know John Denver?" said one of the little girls, leaning on me.

"He look like John Denver," said another.

To start, I needed only to get the nose right. It was slow going, drawing what amounted to BBs on the whole white page. There were no beautiful sweeping strokes, no scratchy sounds of charcoal on rag paper. My audience grew impatient.

"That don't look like him," said one of the little kids.

"I don't see nothin'," said the fat-faced girl.

"Hush up!" said Shanice.

The little girl, leaning against my shoulder, started teasing, "She like you, Jed."

When Shanice slapped her a little too hard on the shoulder, Mrs. Sharpe called her down, and that set in motion so much commotion that everyone except Tyrone, Shanice, and me was sucked out of the room. Then, one by one, the little kids trickled back in and took up a position around me.

"Make me look like Jesse Jackson," Tyrone said, leaning forward, trying to see.

With his nose finally drawn, I could give them something to look at. In dramatic sweeps, I sketched in the cheeks and chin, to their oohs and aahs. To hell with the scratchboard project. This was what art was all about!

Shanice stood closer to me. Her little sister, with big, rolling eyes, noticed.

"She wants you to draw her next, Jed," she said.

"Hey," said Tyrone, with his mother gone, "wanna see my bullet holes?"

Shanice made a groan, and Tyrone lifted up his tank top, showing small circular scars on his fat stomach and ribs. I leaned forward. They looked like burn marks from Granddad's King Edward cigar.

"You got shot?"

"Hell, yeah. Four times."

Four times? How could he not be dead? He could see I was amazed, so he held the shirt up longer for me to see.

Shanice laughed. "You sheltered, boy."

I sat looking at her. So? Maybe I was.

"You don't live in that big fancy house," she said.

"Did it hurt?" I asked Tyrone.

"Duh," Shanice said, hitting me on the shoulder.

"He passed out," laughed one of his little sisters.

Tyrone leaned across the creaky bed, picked up a sneaker, and threw it at her.

"Get, Precious!" he said.

Out of the room, like a flutter of birds, the little ones flew, yapping and carrying on. That left the three of us. Shanice folded her small arms up tight, shifted her weight to one side, and said, "So you come all the way to Bolivar for a 'school project,' huh?"

I knew what she was saying—that Bolivar was second rate to historic Harpers Ferry, where I lived. The only reason anyone ever drove through it was to take a shortcut to the new highway. There were no impressive restored park buildings up here, no tourists, no park rangers, just black families and little streets filled with shotgun houses along busted up sidewalks. Nothing historic or great ever happened here.

"He like you, stupid," said her brother.

I liked how she looked, yes. This was the first time I had seen her without her stupid handkerchief.

"Did you go to Vanessa's?" I said, nodding at her hair.

Vanessa's Hair Salon was the only black hair salon in town, and the only reason I knew about it was that my mother got a kick out of the sign in front: Afronique Braids Available.

"Oh, look," she said to her brother, "now the boy know Bolivar."

Tyrone, rolling out of the bed, crouched over my shoulder like the shadow of a mountain. "You finished, Jed?" When he saw his portrait, it was as if I had given him the world. He grabbed the notebook and ran out of the room, his sister following him.

"I'm gonna sell it," he was saying.

"No, you're not," said Mrs. Sharpe. "You're gonna hang it up."

I was alone in the small room for a moment. I saw a second bed in the corner, along with a sleeping bag along one wall, and another along the opposite wall. They all slept in here? In this tiny room?

Then Shanice came back in. She was strange and quiet and staring at me.

"You really wanna draw me?" she asked.

Her voice was different. All the nastiness was gone. She had the look of having worked up her courage to talk to someone who had just dropped out of outer space. What I would say next, I knew would make a fool of me. But I had always wanted to say it to a girl, and Shanice, suddenly, was the prettiest I had ever seen, even though she was black, and somehow *because* she was black.

"I know my own heart."

I wasn't sure where the saying had come from, maybe a song, but I always liked it. In this case, though, it didn't even sound like my voice. She glanced off as if trying to find the ventriloquist or something. Then her eyebrows went up. "You mean that song? Shasta Q?" When I sat there looking confused, her almond-brown eyes narrowed, and her nasty voice came back. "What you talking about?"

Before I could answer, Tyrone charged back in, acting like an ape, playing an air guitar, twanging out the *Beverly Hillbillies* song.

"Hey, Jed, give me an earring like Eddie Murphy," he said, putting the notebook and pencil back in my hand.

"Don't call him Jed," his sister snapped.

He stopped, his expression froze up, and he started laughing so hard he fell back on his bed.

"Oh, Lordy, Lordy, Lordy, you like him?" he said, rolling around like an idiot. "You like old Jed."

"Shut up!"

"He gonna draw you? He make you white like Farrah Fawcett." He sat up. "Know why they expelled her last year, Jed?"

"Mama!"

"Doing Mr. Jenkins under his desk."

He made a blowjob gesture with his mouth. She slapped at him, but he just covered up and laughed. As she ran out of the room, screaming to her mother, one of her little sisters came in.

"Jed, can I have a drawing, too?" she said, trying to act cute and pretty like Shanice.

A little boy came in behind her. "Can I have a car?"

Behind him was a littler boy with a big open schoolbook teetering in his hands. He dumped it in my lap, trying to hold his finger on a spot on the page.

"Get away, Reginald," said his sister.

"Is this where you from?" he said in his little voice.

It was a map of the United States. All the states were different colors—pink, red, green, blue, yellow. He had his finger on Alabama, which was pink. I said no and moved his finger to West Virginia, which was green.

"No, that's here," he said, in a little voice of protest.

I didn't bother trying to explain that Harpers Ferry was just ten minutes away. Meanwhile, Tyrone was lying on his bed, admiring his drawing. He'd be rich, too, if he could draw like this, he was saying. I stood up. Through the door I could see Mrs. Sharpe at a table heaped with empty Suzy-Q boxes. The rest of the little kids had swarmed outside. I could see them through the small window, carrying on in the bare yard. Shanice was not with them.

I went to the doorway and looked around. Our refrigerator at home was rusting in the same place, and we had a St. Joseph's thermometer on the wall, too. Mrs. Sharpe looked up and saw me looking around.

"Uh, Shanice . . ." I said.

She had the look of a woman who understood immediately.

Behind me, Tyrone got off the creaky bed and came up behind. For the first time, I noticed a trapdoor in the corner of the room and a ladder going down. Mrs. Sharpe nodded, and I started toward it.

"You letting him go down, Mama?" said Tyrone.

I stopped and looked back, my sketchpad in my hands.

"Shanice," the mother called out, "can Jason come down to see you?"

"No!" came her nasty voice through the floor.

Mrs. Sharpe made a gesture for me to go on. As I walked closer to the ladder, Tyrone and his mother came together in the middle of the room. I felt like Neil Armstrong or somebody as I backed down the crude ladder made of two-by-fours.

Below, I could see what looked like a kind of homemade church altar—dozens of pictures of black children on a dresser, surrounded by purple and white candles. Shanice, seeing me coming down, started running her mouth, telling me to get. Her mother yelled down, telling her to behave herself. When I got to the bottom of the ladder, she was standing back by a small bed, looking terrified and infuriated at the same time. My hand slipped off the ladder at the last minute and I almost fell. I was glad. It gave her a reason to laugh. But as soon as I looked around at all the pictures, she yelled for me to leave again. I looked up the ladder for help.

"You just sit down there and draw her," Mrs. Sharpe told me. Then she called down at an angle. "Baby, you can show it to everyone at school, okay?"

Shanice ran her mouth about that, too. I sat down on the bottom step and put the pad on my lap. She stood glaring at me. In the strange light I saw braids in her hair and wondered how she had changed her hairdo so quickly. They made her look tough, like an African warrior. She called me a fool again, and her mother, watching over me from above, told her to get rid of her attitude.

"So?" she said, arms folded. "You just gonna gawk?"

"I need to come closer."

"So come closer!"

I sat on a stool by the dresser, out of view of everyone above.

It was a small, hard, uncomfortable stool, and I sat clinging to my sketchpad, sneaking glances around. The place looked like a bomb shelter made into a bedroom, then into a miniature church. There were more cheap white crucifixes than I could count. Slowly Shanice sat down, too. She was so light her bed barely moved. It was covered with a white lace blanket I could just hear my mother calling lovely.

"You better not make me no white girl," she said. "My boyfriend'll kill you."

I opened my sketchpad, found myself still holding Tyrone's chewed-up pencil, and went into drawing mode.

"What?" she said. "What's wrong with you? Why you looking at me that way?"

"Change . . . change your face."

She cocked her head. "What?"

"You want me to draw you that way? All frowning?"

With effort, she relaxed the hard lines away. From a portrait standpoint, she'd be easy. Her eyes were perfect almonds, her nose was made up of cute round shapes, and her lips were short and full.

"I can put it in a frame for you," I said.

"I don't need no frame. Just draw."

"Who are all these children?"

"None of your business!"

It was hard concentrating. Every time I glanced at her, I found myself looking at her pretty eyes. They were shining right at me. If not her eyes, her smooth brown skin, or her braids. She had a perfect face, like one of the models in my Grumbacher Learn-to-Draw books. Why had I never seen this in school before?

"You better be drawing me, " she said, "not just gawking like a fool."

I started feeling the pressure. I knew that if I didn't make her the prettiest girl in the world, she'd be the maddest. I gave her long eyelashes and lips perfect from corner to corner. Each line and tone had to be right.

"Why you here? You like poor people?" she said. "You ain't gonna get no money for this."

"I know."

I had no answer, and she made a sour remark about that, too. Then she burst out laughing.

"You like Jenny Wilt?"

I tried to act annoyed.

"Yeah, you do," she said, her face filling up with a giggle. "Jed and Jenny."

"Shut up."

She looked surprised that I could be just as sharp-tongued as her.

"You're a trip," she said.

As I glanced at her and drew, I could see her studying me back, making her own portrait of me in her mind.

"Why you act all lonely?" she said.

"What? I don't act lonely."

"Yeah, you do. Like a lonely little dog."

I called her foolish and tried to keep working.

"You scared of something, boy?"

"Shut up."

She laughed again, and then started humming.

"You don't recognize that, fool?"

I stopped, a blank look on my face.

"Duh, 'To Know My Heart'," she said. "Shasta Q? Damn, you dumb."

I went on drawing, ignoring her little putdowns. I worked on her lips, her high cheekbones, the bridge of her nose, adding tone and sharp lines. As hard and nasty as she was on the inside, she was prettier than any white girl I had ever seen.

"Now," I said, sitting up, "how do you want your hair?"

She hopped up off the bed.

"You can draw it the way I want?"

She opened the dresser behind me and started pawing through a heap of wigs—straight brown hair, straight black, brown curls, purplish curls, blonde.

"Turn around," she said.

I stood, pencil and pad in hand, and turned around.

"Okay," she said.

When I turned back around, she had on shoulder-length braids. They made her look like an Egyptian girl.

"What?" she said, not liking the look on my face.

She told me to turn around, which I did, and when I turned back, she had on even longer braids, like strands of beads hanging from a doorway. I shook my head.

"Why?"

"Cause they're for a round face."

"Round face?"

She sighed and gave me an irritated look.

"Turn back around. Damn, you hard to please."

This time when I turned back around, she had on some wild hairdo flipped out at the bottom. I shook my head, she sighed even louder, and back around I turned.

As I waited, I had a chance to look at her bedroom. No posters or pictures of boys. Just pictures of children surrounded by unburned candles. Over her bed was a simple wooden crucifix. It reminded me of my mother's bed.

"Do you know all these kids?" I asked.

"None of your business. Okay, you can look."

I turned around. She had on a long shag.

"Better," I said.

"Better?"

"Something shorter."

She cocked her hips and, with a displeased look, made a little looping motion with her finger for me to turn my back. I didn't understand why she didn't want me to see her changing wigs, but she was being fussy about it.

"Are they relatives?" I asked, my back to her.

"No. Okay, you can turn around."

This time she had on a wavy, collar-length bob she called a bouffant shag. I didn't like shaking my head, but it wasn't exactly right, either.

"Damn, boy!"

I assumed the position and stood looking down at her bed covered with beautiful white lace. I thought she must look like a princess sleeping in it.

"Are you a 'big sister' or something?"

"Why you like Jenny Wilt?" she asked back. "She's just a big flirt."

"She and I were born the same day."

"That ain't why."

"What?"

"Don't turn around!"

I wondered what she was doing that took so long.

"You a virgin?" she laughed.

I was not too scared of her to tell her to fuck off.

"Yeah, you is. Okay, you can turn round."

"No, I'm not either—what's that?" I asked, looking at her latest wig.

Right away she didn't like the look on my face.

"Motown side part—you better like it, boy," she said.

I stepped over to the drawer as if I owned the place. She watched in amazement as I reached into the drawer of wigs myself and picked out a short, dark, curly wig.

"This would look better," I said.

She gave me a suspicious look.

"Why?"

"Cause your face is . . ."

She crossed her arms.

"My face is what?"

"Oval." I waited for her to get nasty, but she didn't. "This'll show more of it," I said.

She gave me a long look.

"Where'd you learn that?" she asked.

I told her about my art book at home, in which it explained how different hair styles complemented, or didn't complement, the face. She burst out laughing, saying I sounded like one of those funny men in hair salons.

"Virgin," she called me again.

"I am not."

"Yeah, you are."

"No, you are," I said.

To that, she gave me such a smug grin that I knew it couldn't possibly be true. It made me sad. I was hoping she was.

We went through a dozen more wigs together. Spiky bangs. Wispy bangs. Bangs plus waves. Wet look. Sassy look. Two-tiered shag. More shoulder-length braids, and even a wild red wig for fun. She had wigs showgirl long, others ooh-la-la short. Even something she called a "face-framing, cascading straw-curl cut," which I thought looked like a big blonde pompom. She was going to be a model, she said. She would need all these wigs in her career.

"You been to the museum on River Street?" I asked.

It was the only way I knew how to say Black History Museum without coming out and saying it, which I didn't feel comfortable saying. She looked at me as if there was no such street. She knew someone on Potomac Street. But she had never heard of River Street.

"They have a famous Afro-Americans gallery," I said.

She cocked me a look. "*Afro*-Americans? Donna Summer there, too?"

I didn't get what was so funny. Speaking of Donna Summer, she had three of her wigs. She showed me. I shook my head to all three.

"This one," I said, pointing back to my original choice.

"Short shag? You wanna see my dumb ole' face, don't ya?" she said, hands on her hips, wig balled up in her hand.

I nodded, and she made the turn-around motion with her little finger. After a few seconds, she said I could look—and boy, did I look.

"Oh, stop getting all google-eyed, boy. You don't have to look at me like no fool."

Her face flashed happiness, embarrassment, confusion, and anger. Some of these looks were wigs, too. I just didn't know which.

"You failing French?" she said. "I bet you are. They gonna hold you back a grade.

"I'm not failing."

"Yes, you is."

"I'm failing art," I said.

She stopped and looked at me. "Art? You? For real?"

I didn't bother trying to explain. I sat down on the stool again.

"Damn, don't get all sad about it, Jed," she said.

She was so hard on me, I almost wanted to laugh. At the same time, the irony was bending in me. She was the prettiest girl I had ever seen, but she was black, and I had picked on her for years behind her back. And to think, I was liking her now.

I thought of my mother, seeing me down in this bomb shelter of a bedroom on Union Street, playing with a black girl's wigs. I could see my brothers behaving no better about it than Tyrone. I saw every white girl in my school looking at me as if I were doing something to offend the race. Why was I turning my back on the timeless rite of liking one of them instead? The answer was simple—none of them liked me.

"Can you come down to the museum with me?" I asked Shanice.

She cocked her head. "You and me, boy? Just walking right down the street? Like we married?"

"My brother will drive us."

"I ain't gettin' down with you," she said, crossing her arms.

My face blushed so hard it felt hot. I had never heard it put this way.

"I know," I said.

She stood looking at me.

"You know?"

I never expected myself to be so agreeable about something that was so far down some impossible road anyway. She gave me a look of curiosity.

"Why you all nice?"

When I shrugged, she shrugged back, to make fun of me.

"Then you'll go?" I said.

She looked off. "If you *ask*, maybe," she said.

I practically leaped through the ceiling.

"Damn, you weird!" she shot back, trying to hold back a smile.

Weird was good. Weird, in this case, was her funky red wig. I reached down into her drawer, grabbed it, and draped it over my head.

"Get that off!" she said, snatching it back and trying to act mad.

I picked up a black wig and plopped that one on my head instead.

"Look, I look just like you," I said.

She stood there shaking her head. I held a blonde wig above her head. "Now you look just like me," I said.

She grabbed it away from me.

"Hey, what about my drawing?"

She made me sit and start drawing again. As I worked, giving her perfect hair, I could feel her looking me up and down.

"All you white boys so short?" she asked. "People gonna look at us in school."

I turned to her. "Hey, does Mr. Romine really live in Bolivar?"

"I don't know. Now why you failing art?"

I had no answer. All I could do was shrug. For that, she stood looking at me, head turned to the side.

"You poor?" she asked.

"No!"

"Then why you wear those old shoes? And those ratty pants?"

"Why you wear that stupid shirt?" I shot back, pointing at its oversized black buttons.

"You act poor, boy."

"Shut up!"

"Ooh, *sensitive* about it, ain't ya?" She turned and looked off. "At least you have self-confidence. Ms. Kerry say I lack it."

"No, you have it."

She turned back to me, surprised I had said this so automatically. I didn't even know what self-confidence was at that moment.

I just wanted her to have what I had. Then, as if I had given her self-confidence, she stood, stepped over to me, and touched my hair. She started smiling, saying how soft it was. She had never touched a white boy's hair before. She stood there for some time, too, pulling every lock to its end, her thin brown arm over my head, blue bracelets clicking together and making a tickling sound in my ears. If my body had been the St. Joseph's thermometer upstairs, I would have burst.

Then she looked down at my drawing.

"Wow, that's me. How'd you do that?" she said, leaning down beside me.

I gave her a little demonstration. With the side of my pencil, I shaded an area of her cheek, then rubbed it with my finger, blending an even tone.

"It's like you putting makeup on me or something."

She squeezed onto the stool beside me, not shy about letting part of her leg touch me. She had perfume on, which made me think of some far-off place.

"Put some here," she said, pointing to a spot on her cheek.

"No, it has to be natural," I said.

"Here."

The graphite on my fingertip made a soft tone across her forehead. If I had been drawing a white face, I would have left the area white. Suddenly, she took hold of my hand and turned my finger up to see the pencil graphite on the tip. Then she looked over my whole hand, as if looking for the magic in it.

"You'd be rich doing this," she said.

"That'd be nice," I said, my voice dropping off.

She looked over. "You are poor, ain't ya?"

"Kinda."

Her forehead pulled up in soft wrinkles, like ridges in the sand.

"Over in fancy *Happers* Ferry?" she said. "For real?"

I nodded and looked around the basement. I was the only white face in this room, in this house, and on this street. Maybe the only white face in this whole town. That meant my little white secret could come out. My family probably had the worst house in historic Harpers Ferry—run-down, embarrassing, and hickish. Ordinarily this was no big deal because there were always black people in Bolivar to put down first. But with me here and with all the whites across town, lies didn't matter. They were like a suitcase full of Confederate money.

"So where do you live?"

I braced for impact. "Hog Alley."

"Hog Alley!" Her voice shot up. "You're kidding? Which house?"

"The yellow one."

"Down by all them boxcars and that huge pile of coal?"

I nodded, and she shot to her feet. "That place with no windows?"

"It has windows."

"No, it don't." She jabbed her finger into my shoulder. "That place is a dump!"

I laughed so hard that, fearing that the whole house had heard me, I scrunched down and put my hand to my mouth, acting all silly.

"That's a nasty old house, Jed!" She pushed me off the stool and onto the floor—sketchpad, pencil, and all. "You're a snob, Jason Stevens!" She started pinching and poking at me, and I was laughing and trying not to pee myself. "My mother got cancer, and you all looking down on people," she said, digging into my stomach.

"What?" I said, pushing her hands away and sitting up. I was trying not to laugh now. I climbed to my feet. "What, Shanice?"

"Ovarian," she said in a low voice, with a glance toward the ladder.

I took half a step closer. "Serious?"

She nodded. "She seen three specialists already."

The planet stopped turning, the house went dark, and my mind folded down to one thought—death. It wasn't about Harpers Ferry or Bolivar anymore, or whose house was nasty looking, and it certainly wasn't about art class or even whether I'd fail for the year. The worst part of all, it wasn't even about her mother's cancer, either, which it should have been. It was about how mixed up we both were and how every stupid thing always ended up being devastating.

Then Shanice did something incredible—she threw her arms around me. It was a strong, beautiful hug that squeezed my shoulder blades so hard my arms popped out straight. As quickly, she let go, sat down on the stool, looked off in the opposite direction, and, with her arms draped over her knees, started rocking herself back and forth. When I took too long to put my arm around her, she smacked at me. I deserved that. How to touch someone when it really mattered—this was something my brother's dirty magazines never taught. And the only time my mother ever touched my father was when he wanted Caladryl on his back.

Tyrone didn't know about the cancer, she said, sniffing. No one at her church knew, either. Her mother only told her because she was the oldest. As I sat listening, the moment seemed unreal, and I was trying to catch up. She broke into tears, but as quickly her voice rose up in rage.

"My mama already had one surgery, and now it's back!"

My grandmother had three surgeries, I said, and every time her cancer came back.

I had another chance to hold her, but again my arms were lame. When Shanice turned to me, glassy-eyed, I knew what she was thinking: She may have been poor and black and from Bolivar, but she knew how to put her arms around someone when it mattered.

When I said that maybe her mother would get better, she said that less than 1 percent survived after the second surgery. She said that some girl at school had a cousin who died in a hospice after three surgeries and two years of chemo.

I watched her step over to her bed, sit down on it with a bounce, fall over on her side, and curl up like a child. I started toward her, but she popped up first.

"So why you come here?" she asked one final time, talking a step toward me. "You never talk to me in school."

I didn't like her icy smile or her tone. She knew very well why. Because of my stupid school assignment. That, and what I told her earlier.

But she shifted those damn killer hips again. "Oh, you just come up here by yourself because you 'know your own heart'? No other reason? You as disgusting as me," she said, flouncing past.

"You're crazy."

"No, I ain't," she said, rounding her bed and bouncing down on the other side of it. "You disgusting, and you know it. I know your house now."

I stood glaring at her for the longest time, then turned away. Thousands of kids blurred in my eyes. White crosses did zigzags in the air. She was right. I was disgusting. I didn't feel good enough to set foot in one house over in Harpers Ferry. Not one! I had searched every street before coming here, looking for just one door to knock on. I walked past fancy house after fancy house, not feeling worthy of approaching one. I ended up two miles up the road, where people wouldn't look down on me.

Slowly I walked back over to Shanice and sat down on her bed with her.

"So I guess we're in the same boat," I said.

"No," she said, throwing my arm off her, "you in a worse one."

She hopped up and pulled her shirt down snug, saying she hoped she didn't get cooties from me. No telling what she might pick up from my ugly old house over in Harpers Ferry.

I was back to glaring again. Nothing worked with her. Not kindness. Not anger. As soon as I thought something was happening between us, she blew up in my face. I couldn't tell her she was pretty. She'd only get angry and slap at me. I couldn't tell her she was an angry bitch. She'd slap me for sure then.

"Your mama raised you," she said. "That's your problem. Made you like a girl."

That was one hell of a remark even from her.

"I was sick when I was younger," I said. "Okay? It's not my fault."

She looked back at me. "Sick?"

"Almost died," I said, turning away.

"For real?"

She started closer. I didn't want to tell her the truth, that I only had a wicked cold, but I had set up something dramatic. I had to deliver.

"Fever. 108."

"108!"

"Almost caused brain damage," I said.

She came over and sat back down beside me. Her little brother Germaine was sick all the time, too. Fevers, earaches, colds. He spent a whole week in the hospital once, she said.

I spent two whole weeks in a hospital in Baltimore. The nurses gave us Curious George books. We watched Joe Bazooka boxing movies. I was in a large room with all kinds of sick kids—blind kids, kids with no arms, kids with cancer, all of us mixed in together. The kid beside me had no legs, I said. His name was Win. I thought that was strange. The unluckiest boy in the world named Win? He bothered me the whole week, asking me to un-lock the combination lock on his luggage.

"I still think about him."

Shanice looked at me as if I was the most pathetic kid in the world.

"You too shy," she said, feeling my curls.

When I looked at her, something in my face disappointed her again. She stood and stepped off.

"Why you all that way?" she said, looking back, her face all strained up.

She didn't know the half of it. In the picture window of the wax museum across the street from my house stood a big figure of John Brown, all done up in fury, thrusting a musket. All our lives he had been glaring at our house. We always figured he was enraged with our racist father. In a town famous for being where black freedom started, Dad was begging for it.

"I guess we all a little poor," she finally said. "You have a phone?"

"No."

"Me neither. TV?"

"Yeah."

"We do, too."

I picked up the notepad, sat, and started working again, with her quietly beside me. I wanted to tell her she was easy to make beauti-ful on paper. She was already beautiful. All I had to do was copy her.

"He looks like my cousin," I said, pointing at the picture of a boy on the end of the dresser.

"What, you have a black cousin?" she laughed.

His name was Anthony McDonald, she said, standing. I stood with her, and together we stood looking at the pictures. There must have been fifty.

"They all kids killed in the U.S. this year," she said.

I was afraid to ask how. Drive-by shootings. Abuse. Malnutrition.

"You ever light these candles?" I asked.

"I want to," she said. "But Mama say I'd burn the house down." She pointed to a little girl missing her baby teeth. "That's Shanice. Her name Shanice, too."

Standing beside her, I could hear the happiness in her voice. Shanice was a cool name, I said. All the girls down in Harpers Ferry were named Sarah or Emily.

"I go by Shani to my friends," she said.

"Shani," I said.

I pointed at an older boy in a suit.

"Who's he?"

"Brandon Carr."

She named the two boys beside him, Luther Washington and Justin Mennefee, then went on naming them by their first name—*David, Kayla, Jasmine, Destiny.* I looked over at her. She had a strange, peaceful smile.

The names went on and on—*Briana, Ashley, Michael, Anthony.* All these smiling little faces—a boy with a ball cap, a girl our age, another toddler. All black and all dead. All dead as if because they were black. Suddenly I felt very tired, and a sick feeling ran through me. I had to sit down.

"Now what's wrong with you?" she snapped.

"Nothing."

"Why you all red-eyed?"

"I'm not."

"You don't know them."

Still, I was sad, so sad I had to sit down.

"You asked me who they was," she said, getting upset.

"I know." I glanced back at the ladder.

"Go ahead, leave."

I wanted to. I wanted out of this basement funeral home, this mausoleum. How could she sleep down here with all these dead kids looking at her? It was as if she was trying to be their mother or something, when her own mother was dying from cancer. It was too morbid to stand.

"Ain't my fault they dead," she said, getting more upset.

I was weird, she said, and her boyfriend was going to kill me for being down here, and she wouldn't go with me to a museum if I was the last boy on earth.

"My mama the one dying!" she all but shouted, her face raked down to the bone in anguish, pictures of dead children ringing her.

"I know," I pleaded back. "Your mother should talk to my mother."

She looked tripped up by this and let out an ugly laugh. "Your mother?"

Yes! After dealing with our grandmother's illness for years, my mother could talk cancer the way I could talk baseball. All of us, even my stupid brothers and hard-ass father, after seeing Grandma turn yellow from cancer and the skin fall off her bones, would have the hearts of Mother Teresa for this family.

But Shani wanted to fight more. "When your mama ever come over into Bolivar?"

It was hopeless. There was too much garbage between us. All I saw was black, and all she saw was white.

"Your mama think we're trash," she went on.

"So don't act like it."

I caught her hand coming for my face just in time and threw it away like balled up paper.

"I hate you!" she hissed.

Just then, Tyrone's big black arm came down from above, yanked off her wig, and disappeared up the ladder with it. She screamed and tried to cover her head with her hands, but not before I saw the ugly white scar across her scalp and the mangled hair growing around it. I couldn't take my eyes off it. It was the ugliest sight—hair and white skin smeared together as if her head was made of melted wax. And where there wasn't a scar or messed up hair, there were pasted down cornrows that made her head like a boy's.

She screamed at me to stop gawking, stomped her feet in a crazy fit, all while trying to grab another wig from the drawer. But she ended up putting on the funny red wig, which made the moment worse. She shrieked for me to get out, threw the notebook at me, but hit her dead children pictures instead, scattering them on the floor like cards. Then she really went berserk, flailing her arms, whimpering. I stood petrified. She was like those retarded children in my school who jumped up and down on their desks and peed themselves. When her mother yelled down, wanting to know what was going on, I went on autopilot.

"No, it's okay, it's okay," I called up, doing my best to sound calm. "I'm not finished yet. It's okay."

I looked over at Shani and put my finger to my lips. She stood backed up against her bed, half angry, half confused. I picked up the pad and pencil, sat down on the stool again, and started erasing. Before she could scream out that I was ruining her drawing, I put my finger to my lips again. She quickly put on another wig and started gathering up all her precious pictures and putting them back in place on the dresser.

"Shani?" her brother called down.

"Get, Ty," she said, her wet eyes transfixed on my hands.

"You okay, baby?" her mother called down.

"Yeah," she said, in a distracted voice, stepping closer to see.

The best thing about Tyrone's stupid, chewed-up pencil was its big, soft eraser. Spinning the pad on my lap like a piece of pottery, I quickly erased her hair. Keeping the lightest pressure, I was careful not to rough up the texture of the paper. Several times I stopped to blow the paper clean and to turn the eraser to a fresh side.

Out of the corner of my eye, I saw her coming closer. Since I looked like an expert, she wouldn't have another conniption.

"It's okay, it's okay," I kept saying, smiling and nodding.

My heart was pounding for the life of me. I was scared of her, but embarrassed for her, too, and crazy about her all at the same time. She drove pain into me, then knocked it out like a hammer knocking nails out of lumber.

With her hair erased away, I started drawing in cornrows. Another girl in my class had them, so I knew just how they looked. I built little rows of rounded lines. I worked quickly, too, not sure how long I had before she would go crazy again or her mother would call down. Where she had her terrible scar, I drew in full, dark, beautiful braids, flat to the scalp, in perfectly spaced rows around her pretty face. Out of the corner of my eye, I could see her peering over my shoulder.

"Don't make 'em too thick," she said.

"I won't," I promised.

She sat down beside me again.

"How you do that?" she said, sniffing.

"I don't know," I said.

"Talent," she said, answering herself.

"My father painted when he was younger."

She looked over.

"But you ain't close to your father?" Her voice was different—light and weak from her little spell.

I shook my head.

"My father hit me," she said.

I looked at her. I couldn't dare kiss her. I couldn't even say something sweet. All I could do was wish.

"Put more here," she said, pointing to a spot.

I nodded and laid the pencil on its side and gave the paper an extra shot of tone. She was tired of wearing wigs, she said. She had to wear them for the rest of her life.

"When?" she said, sniffing.

I looked at her. Her face was relaxed, and she was gazing at the drawing with wonder.

"When what?"

"When are we going? I can go tomorrow—wait," she said, turning to me on the little stool, "what am I gonna see?" She sat with her arms crossed, as if her little fit had left her chilled.

"Paintings," I said.

She looked disappointed again.

"Any pictures?"

"Some."

"Least they got that," she said. I could feel her looking me up and down. "Why you wanna go with me? You can't hold hands with me or nothing."

"Maybe not out in public," I said.

If she could feel my hand, then I could hold her hand. I stopped drawing and took hold of it. It was soft and small. I touched one of her long blue fingernails.

"You're silly," she said, sniffing. She saw me look over at the pictures. "The church gives them out. I just started collecting them. Somebody got to remember them. You gonna let go of my hand?"

On the edge of her bed was a six-subject Mead notebook as

thick as a dictionary. I had seen only one before. The smartest kid in our school carried one.

"Can I look?"

She nodded.

With its deep blue cover and embossed silver logo, it was the opposite of her brother's flimsy notebook with a goofy, canary-yellow cover. On the inside cover was

Shanice L. Sharpe
Harpers Ferry High
10th Grade

I told her she had the prettiest handwriting and ran my fingers over the letters as if they were precious beads. *Analysis of the production, distribution, and consumption of goods and services is the chief concern of economy as a social science.* Pages and pages of beautiful handwriting. No doodling in the margins, no angry marks, nothing sloppy or silly. In the back, on a page by itself, I caught a glimpse of a poem. In that second, I memorized every word.

Someday I'll fly like the bird I can not see.
Someday I'll love like the heart I can not feel.
Someday I'll smile like the face I have not seen.

Lights were sparkling in the corners of my eyes, and my body felt like a hot air balloon I couldn't keep down. With all my heart I wished I was black, or she was white, or we could stay down here forever.

"Your mom miss your grandma?" she asked.

I nodded. Life, I thought, was like finger-painting with a hopeless mess of gruesome colors. You kept smudging it around until you got it right.

"What kind of cancer she have?"

I couldn't remember exactly, and that seemed to disappoint her. She looked down at her notebook on my lap.

"Ms. Kerry say I have self-esteem issues—why you smiling like that?"

A black girl could be my first. That was why I was smiling. And if that could happen, anything could. A UFO could land on my head, or my scratchboard project could hang in the National Gallery.

Shani just didn't know how pretty and smart she was, just as Tyrone didn't know what to do with all his size.

"You can be a model," I said, "if you have the guts to do that."

I nodded at the shrine of pictures on her dresser. If she could collect pictures of dead children and sleep with them staring at her all night long, then she was the coolest, bravest person I had ever met. She could move anywhere, become anyone. I told her so, and all anger went out of her eyes.

"You serious?"

"If you can do that," I said.

She looked down.

"I've never been to a museum before," she said, looking down.

I shrugged. It was okay that she lived in Bolivar but had never been down in Harpers Ferry. I had lived in Harpers Ferry all my life but had never been here, I said. She didn't seem to hear, though. She was looking down at the drawing of her with perfect cornrows.

"I know why you draw."

"Why?"

She didn't answer. She just smiled and put her head on my shoulder. I stopped working, and we sat still. Seconds stretched out into minutes. Some time later, there were footsteps above.

"Baby," her mother called down, "we going to the new Kmart. You wanna come?"

Shani turned her head up to the ceiling. "No."

Silence came back down at us. Long seconds of it. I could feel her mother peering down at another angle, trying to see what we were up, too. We sat perfectly still on the stool, holding hands, our fingers making sweat in the crevices.

"You sure, baby?"

Shani exploded on her. "Yeah! He still drawin' me, okay?"

It was a boom to put an end to all nosy mothers. Then she looked at me, grinned, and put her finger to her lips. Another eternity of quiet passed.

"Okay then," her mother said, moving off. Then she stopped. "Goodbye, Jason—say hello to your mother for me."

I let go of Shani's hand, went to ladder, and looked up.

"Goodbye, Mrs. Sharpe," I called up.

But she had already moved away.

Upstairs, kids were running in circles, shaking the floor. Doors were being slammed, and Ty was causing trouble. The idiot yelled down to us—"Don't do nothin' I would do!" First time the big galoot was funny. But Shani didn't smile, just told him to shut up.

More door slamming, more house shaking, more hitting and squabbling. Finally, after a stampede down the outside steps, shaking the whole rickety house like a tree house—quiet. It filled this basement room and settled on all the pictures like the tranquility of evening time. Wigs lay everywhere as though Shani and I had flung off our clothes in great passion for each other. Finally, through the old boards of the house came the sound of a car with no muffler popping to life.

As it pulled off, she and I sat looking at each other. Around us, the walls rose up with a glow from upstairs. It made me think of a night sky over us.

"I haven't been with a boy either," she said. "Not the right way, anyway." She scooted closer and sat with her legs under her. "You wanna see my nipple ring?"

As I nodded, I felt her eyes hook into mine. I watched her unbutton her shirt, her thin, black fingers climbing down the front like a spider. She lifted her moon-white bra over one breast. It was small and brown, and the ring on her nipple, catching the light from above, was a gold angel inside a sunburst. I didn't have time to get excited or think about what I was seeing.

"You can touch it," she said.

She rose up on her knees and leaned over me so that her breast was directly level with my eyes. Angel, nipple, and breast bounced like a Christmas tree ornament to the touch of my finger.

"It's beautiful," I said, looking up at her.

Her eyes were full with a thousand glints. She sat back slump-shouldered for a moment, then unbuttoned her shirt the rest of the way, and looked at me with the blankest, matter-of-fact expression.

Generations

***

I woke that morning to a sight drawing me up in fear—my father standing over my bed.

"Come on, get up," he said. "You're going with me today. Your mother's already packed you a lunch."

I was confused and sullen before even awake. My father had been coming to the house more often recently. Apparently he and Mom were patching things up.

"You wanted to see *Worsh*-ington," he said, looming over me. "Well, I'm gonna show you the capital. Get up."

Stumbling downstairs to get away from him, I found Mom in the kitchen.

"Jason," she said quietly, "just go along with it."

"But, Mom, I have French!"

Dad was right behind me.

"You can miss one day," he growled.

The bastard had to order me to eat breakfast, order me to get dressed, and then order me out into the car, which, I discovered, was already piled high with mail for the day.

My father was the last of the rural letter carriers in our county opting to use his own personal vehicle to deliver the mail. It was legal, as long as he kept his emergency flashers on and a mail sign in the back window. But talk about embarrassing—Dad pulling over to mailboxes around town in our family car.

Apparently, this morning, he had gone to the post office early, loaded up, and stopped back here for me. What did he have planned? To stick me into a mailbox somewhere to get rid of me? I was sure this had something to do with my grandfather's "influence" on me.

As we pulled out of town, I scooted down in the seat so as not to be seen, our crappy little car vibrating and groaning as if about to self-destruct. This, believe it or not, was an official U.S. mail car, but with 207,000 miles on this engine alone, it was a contraption of shimmies and rattles.

Once on the highway, Dad stayed in the slow lane, emergency blinkers on. In this repainted red Oldsmobile station wagon that tilted to one side, on account of a bad shock, we looked like a big bloody bandage limping down the road. We went past where the school bus usually turned around and on past where Mom shopped. Out here, past the new Montgomery Ward store and the Evans Chevrolet dealership, along with a McDonald's, Wendy's, and Burger King all within half a mile—the eastern panhandle of West Virginia was at its worst.

"Look, there's the damn *Worsh*-ington Monument," he said, pointing at the long neck of the Citgo gas sign.

Out of the corner of my eye, I saw him waiting for me to grin.

"It's *Wash*-ington," I said back, "not *Worsh*-ington!"

I hated how hicks around here pronounced it.

"And there's the White House," he went on, pointing at the new Chesapeake Bay Seafood House.

He wasn't funny, the bastard.

"Look, the Lincoln Memorial!" I shouted, lunging my arm at the Ponderosa Steakhouse and following it up with the ugliest look.

"Jason," he said, over the noisy air ruffling through the cracked windows, "what in the hell's gotten into you lately?"

He named everything I was doing wrong with my life—failing my classes, hanging around with blacks from Bolivar, running up to see my "grandfather," who, in his opinion, wasn't really my grandfather, but the goofy person my mother's mother had remarried.

"Why can't you be more like your brothers?" he said.

I looked out the window. What, loser doofuses?

"I say to your damn mother, 'Katie, why can't Greg help that son of yours pass English?'"

French, idiot.

"Know what she says?"

No, what, jerk?

"'Well, Bill, they're different.' Different? 'In different grades,' she says."

Out of the corner of my eye, I saw him looking over at me.

"Your mother and I," he went on, suddenly trying to sound decent, "were always at odds on how to raise you kids, even though I tried—"

"Look!" I shouted over his voice, pointing at the flaking old billboard for Howard Johnson's. "The U.S. Capitol Building!"

When he raised his hand to slap me, I pulled one of the mail bags between us. He cussed and threatened for a while, but for the moment, I got the last laugh.

Seven miles out, we took the Jefferson Parkway exit. Wide lanes, bright yellow dashes, shiny reflectors, grassy area in between—looked like an airport runway. Here he pulled over and told me to get in the backseat. From this point on, he had to drive from the passenger side of the car.

No kidding. Since he chose to use his personal vehicle to deliver mail, rather than a standard mail van with right-side steering, he had to drive from the passenger side. That way, he could shove mail into boxes as he pulled up, like a normal carrier using a van. Apparently, it was legal. The cops left him alone anyway. And according to my father, this kind of driving had actually been a job requirement of letter carriers in the old days. He could do it too. He just reached his leg over the hump in the floor and worked the gas and brake like nobody's business, all while steering with his left hand.

So I got in the backseat with the mail bags, and he pulled on, from the passenger side. Soon everyone barreling past us did a double take—we looked like Jalopy Driving School with an invisible student. You'd be surprised how far down into a Oldsmobile station wagon you can slide when you're mortified enough.

On his morning run alone, he had fifty-six stops to make, or 172 addresses he was responsible for getting the mail to. The old car groaned from one fancy housing development to another, places called Cherry Acres Estates and Huntington Acres. The damn post office, he didn't mind griping along the way, was supposed to have phased-in two more carriers on this route alone, but nothing ever happened, thanks to red tape. That left him overworked, with the union not standing behind him.

Inside these posh developments, most mailbox islands were empty, since it was mid-morning, but at some, nice cars were pulling up just as Dad was shoving pieces of mail into boxes that looked like shiny safety-deposit boxes. I sank down into the seat while Dad went into his "personality routine." Became all smiles and pleasantries. In those few minutes, as he put on performance after performance to rich people who merely gave him amused glances, I knew he had the worst job in the world, if not the worst life.

At 12:01 by the big Jefferson Savings Bank sign, Dad stopped right along the highway to eat his bag lunch, emergency flashers clicking, new cars barreling past, shoving our old car with jolts of air.

"Let me tell you something about your grandfather," he started by saying, still sitting on the passenger side, now looking across the car, legs partly up on the seat. To traffic flying by, we looked like a family of three broken down, the driver out walking to a service station somewhere.

"There's nothing special about him," he said, eating his sandwich by peeling back the plastic baggy, never touching the bread with his fingers. "Roy just likes the easy life."

I had heard this before. He always had to *tell me something* about the man Grandma married, something to pin him down and ruin him once and for all.

Roy didn't tinker on one car forever or sit in the sunshine all afternoon whittling a stick. He preferred his air-conditioned living room and RCA TV. He even had a bird feeder, kept a clean yard, put storm windows on the house, and waved to his neighbors. Also, he was a northern Democrat—good only for raising daughters.

"You'll never be like him," my father said on this occasion. "So don't even try."

"I know. I'm not, and I don't wanna be," I said right back.

He looked back at me, but I kept from giving him any explanation, any clue, as to who I might want to be like now. Then he turned, looked out into the middle of nowhere, and started reminiscing. Years ago, he said, when this land was dotted with stone farmhouses and round barns, he was often scouting around for good junk for the taking. He didn't need to remind me. How many times he came home with something heaped up in the backseat, some plank of decorative walnut or unusual assembly of what looked like scrap iron but he insisted was old and valuable. Times, though, had changed. All around now were the greenest, picture-perfect expanses of transplanted grass, stabbed with shiny steel power line poles—pins through the broken heart of the earth. He'd find no more old junk lying about out here to take. The world had moved beyond him.

"Your damn mother," he said, looking over the seat at me, "has it in her head that you're like me! But I told her, no way, you're *nothing* like me."

Nothing, indeed.

"And another thing, while we're on your mother. I'm none too happy that that damn Lonny Dunn is now working maintenance at town hall, so damn close to your grandmother."

He glared back at me as if I had something to do with that.

"She seems to have some damn friendship with him . . . I can't understand it."

He went into his old song that he had grown up with catechism and discipline, both of which my brothers and I lacked. Then he glanced back at me.

"Where's your sketchpad?"

"Home."

"Home?"

He proceeded to grab a few pieces of junk mail, collect them into the thickness of a tablet, top it off with a piece of rag-weave paper from a brown shopping bag, and wrap the whole contraption with a rubber band. Then he slapped a pencil on top and handed it over the backseat, saying, "Here, sketch with this."

He was serious, too. Never mind that I'd be drawing on the

back of an A&P bag, rather than in my Grumbacher, sixty-pound-paper, fine-line sketchpad.

Some time in the hot afternoon, during all the endless stops at the same-looking housing developments, I fell half-asleep with my face in a musty canvas mail bag. In the back of my mind was nothing good at all. More and more it seemed I would die before reaching sixteen. I mean, what was wrong with a trip to the nation's Capital? To the National Zoo? To the Smithsonian to figure out the origin of, like, life?

"Jason," my father said, rousing me, "I want to tell you something."

As I raised my head, the vibration of the car filled the silence after his voice.

"Your damn grandfather sent you a piece of mail."

I looked over the seat at the side of his head. A piece of mail?

"Didn't 'send' it," he went on. "Came by the post office this morning and asked me to give to you. *Me?* Anyway, it's around here somewhere." He glanced around the dash and seat in a phony effort to locate it. I was already looking too. "I don't know what in the hell he has in mind for you." This he made sound as if I should know. "But I'm gonna leave the whole matter up to your mother." He glanced up in the mirror. "He's *her* damn relation."

I spotted an envelope with granddad's handwriting on it in the corner of the dash. With sunlight on it, I could see even from the backseat the faint shape of a blue Amtrak ticket inside—a ticket to Washington, just as granddad had promised!

I looked at my father.

"Keep sketching," he said.

And just like that, nothing else would be said about it. I would sit in this car for another hour in curiosity, then in my room half the evening, wondering what kind of father I had.

Acknowledgments

***

Grateful acknowledgment is made to the journals in which these stories first appeared: *Northwords, Rosebud, The Bitter Oleander, Confrontation, Concho River Review, Salt River Review, Oyez Review, The Foliate Oak, Global City Review, Passager, The Cortland Review, The Iowa Review,* and *Stirring: A Literary Collection.* Special gratitude is given to the following journal editors: Moira Forsyth, Paul B. Roth, Martin Tucker, Terry Dalrymple, Mary Azrael, Kendra Kopelke, Ginger Murchison, and David Hamilton. A heartfelt thank you goes to my agent, Penny Nelson, and to this collection's editor, Hilary Attfield, for their belief in these stories. Special thanks to Susan Smollens and graduate editor Rachel King for their fine editing. My sincere appreciation goes to the entire staff of West Virginia University Press for their invaluable work in publishing this collection—and for welcoming me as a native writer.

John Michael Cummings is a short story writer and novelist. He is the prize-winning author of *The Night I Freed John Brown*.